MW01028931

FREE DIVE

Dive deep...
— Emma Shelford

FREE DIVE

BOOK ONE
OF THE
NAUTILUS LEGENDS

EMMA SHELFORD

This is a work of fiction. Names, characters, places, and incidents either are the product of the author's imagination or are used factitiously, and any resemblance to any persons, living or dead, business establishments, events, or locales is entirely coincidental.

FREE DIVE

Kinglet Books
Victoria BC, Canada

ISBN: 978-1999101909

www.emmashelford.com

First edition: June 2019

DEDICATION

For all the scientists who inspired and supported me.

MATHIAS

Mathias Nielsen throttled down the engine of his motorboat. Thick fog muffled the noise and made it echo as if in a small, gray room. The shore loomed darkly ahead like a leviathan from the deep. A long dock bisected gently lapping waves. It was a rickety thing, half-eaten away by barnacles, salt, and waves, but sturdy enough to support a shadowy figure standing at the end, scarcely visible in the swirling mists. A foghorn sounded, low and melancholy, in the distance.

Matt's fingers twitched on the steering wheel in nervous anticipation. This was it, the first step in his plan. He had high hopes, even though it was a long shot. But, like his grandfather always said, fish or cut bait. His girlfriend Bianca deserved more than he could provide on his meager deckhand salary. There wasn't a lot he could do in Sayward, not with his limited qualifications. Turns out crewing private sailboats in the Pacific for a decade didn't offer many transferable skills.

When the motorboat was close enough, Matt pulled up to the dock with practiced ease and threw the painter over the side of the dock. The shadowy figure, now resolved as a pot-bellied man with thinning gray hair, secured it. Matt jumped onto the wooden platform.

"Larry Eastman?" he said.

"The one and only." Larry thrust out his hand in friendly greeting. Matt grasped it and shook firmly. "Tom told me you wanted this." Larry nudged a Styrofoam container on the dock beside him. "And were willing to pay good money for it. How could I say no?"

Tom Banks, a mutual acquaintance, had a love of beer that was only exceeded by his love of gossip. It hadn't taken many drinks before Tom had told Matt all about his buddy

Larry's bizarre bycatch and the shenanigans that followed. Matt, whose mind was never far from money-making schemes these days, had immediately seen the possibilities.

"Glad you felt that way," Matt said. He gestured to the container. "Can I see it?"

"Be my guest. Just don't touch it unless you're ready for a ride. Tried it on me and my buddies a few times. It was wild. People will line up for that." Larry bent down and lifted a corner of the lid. Matt leaned over and peered inside. The container shuddered with movement, and he jumped back. Larry laughed.

"Yep, it's a frisky one."

"What kind of fish is it? Any ideas?"

"Hell if I know. Some messed-up salmon, I guess. But not really. Nothing I've seen before, and I've fished these parts for thirty years. But if you wanted to catch another one, go to the north end of Harwood Island and use this as bait." Larry held open a plastic shopping bag so Matt could look inside. "I dropped a bit into the bucket and the fish went berserk. Loved it."

Matt looked at the bait inside the bag with incredulity. If it worked, though, he wouldn't say a word against it. Having only one fish was a major hole in his plan. If it died, he would have nothing. With more, not only would he have a safeguard, but he could ramp up production. A smile crept across his severe features before he could suppress it.

"Got big plans, hey?" Larry patted him familiarly on the shoulder. "If I were a younger man, I'd think about joining you. But for the right amount of cash, I'm just as happy leaving the mystery to you. You're a young guy, fill of piss and vinegar. You'll figure it out." Larry grinned. "Or figure out how to make some coin off it."

"Here's the money, as agreed," Matt said. He passed Larry a thick envelope. It hurt to let go of the cash, but it took money to make money. If this gamble worked, it would pay

2

off big time. He thought of the bait and frowned, then he slowly pulled out his wallet and thumbed a few bills from it. He passed them to Larry. "Plus a little extra. So you don't feel the need to tell anyone else about the bait."

Larry winked at him.

"Say no more. My lips are sealed."

The container shuddered with movement when Matt picked it up, but he wedged it firmly under a seat. As he roared off, he pulled out his phone to text his cousin Pete.

I got the fish. Buy the equipment. We're on.

CORRIE

Corrie Duval flicked her dark brown ponytail over her shoulder to get it out of the way. She'd have to remember to tuck it under her lab coat to avoid it contaminating her work. She looked at her immaculate lab bench, every beaker, pen, and pipette in its place. Her sampling equipment lay in neat rows on the bench. It was tidy, but it still irked Corrie that the equipment marred the smooth expanse of counter. She would have to pack it in her bag soon to clean up.

"What else do I need for sampling tomorrow?" she asked Daniel, her lab mate. He was in the last year of his doctorate, so she turned to him as the font of all knowledge. When he didn't look angrily busy, that is.

"Did you book the department truck?" he said without unfolding his lanky frame from the microscope. "Unless you have your own car. Truck's easier, though."

"Yep, got it."

"Carboys, refractometer, thermometer?"

"Thermometer! Thanks, Daniel." Corrie walked a step then stopped.

"Top shelf," Daniel said with a tone of patient resignation.

"Thanks."

Corrie spotted the case of thermometers. She reached up, but even on tiptoes, it was too far for her to grab.

"I hate being short," she grumbled. A nearby stepstool provided her with a boost, and she laid a thermometer on the lab bench beside two large plastic jugs for holding water. She checked her watch then jumped.

"Damn it! I'm late for my meeting with Jonathan."

"He's always late," said Daniel. "Don't stress."

True to Daniel's word, Dr. Jonathan Chang's office door was closed when Corrie skidded to a halt before it and knocking yielded no result. A minute later, her supervisor strolled down the hall, his bald head gleaming under the fluorescent lights.

"Ah, Corrie. Good." He unlocked the door. "Come on in."

Corrie sat gingerly on the edge of a wooden chair while Jonathan shuffled papers around on his desk between them. Her fingers itched to sort the mess on his desk, and she sat on them to avoid the impulse.

"So," he said finally. "Have you progressed on thoughts for your project? We had a few ideas you wanted to explore last time. What looks like the most promising, given your reading of the scientific literature?"

"I'd like to focus on the metabolomics of bacteria in white plumose anemones. There has been some research into the anti-cancer compounds that they produce. I'd like to study both that, and whether environmental conditions affect metabolite production. That could really help if someone decides to produce the compounds in a lab."

Jonathan nodded slowly and steepled his hands.

"It's an interesting area of study, and certainly, not well-researched. But I sense some hesitancy. Is there something else you want to look into?"

Corrie tried not to grimace. She knew what she would study if it were completely up to her. It wouldn't fly, though. Not in a million years. But there were other interesting things to study that were still academically acceptable.

"What I would really like to do," said Corrie. "Is to examine the bacterial phylogenetic tree using metagenomics, and maybe find a new species. Do different strains produce varied compounds in different conditions? I'm sure they could teach us much more about bacterial evolution."

Jonathan chuckled.

"Everyone wants to discover a new species. You have a name picked out already, don't you? Let me caution you against making that your sole goal—new species tend to be found by serendipity, not searching. But I like it, you're on

5

the right track. Start sampling."

By the time Corrie left Jonathan's office, she was an odd mixture of deflated and elated. Finally, after six months of her masters' program, she had a working project idea. She hoped her first solo sampling excursion tomorrow was successful. She had science to do.

ZEBALLOS

Zeballos Artino kicked the sandals off his dusky bare feet and threw himself onto the sand. The ocean glittered under a spring sun that had peered out today after two weeks of incessant rain. The undersides of the driftwood logs that piled along the shore were still damp, but the top layer of sand was dry enough to sit on.

His friend, Jules Elliot, sat with a log at his back and his arms draped over relaxed bent legs. He brushed shaggy brown hair out of his eyes and reached into a paper bag to twist the cap off a bottle hidden inside.

"It's a bit cliché, isn't it? Liquor in a brown bag?" Zeb watched Jules through pale-gray eyes, half-closed against the bright sun.

"Cliché for a reason, my friend. Keeps the cops off our backs." Jules held up the bag. "To your dad. May he rest in peace. Or, failing that, may he party on with all the interesting people down below."

Jules took a swig, grimaced, and passed the bottle to Zeb. He took it and drank down a mouthful before he could think too hard about why they were drinking. He managed not to cough, but it was a close thing. Jules had bought cheap tequila, barely a step up from drain cleaner. Zeb took another swig and passed the bottle back. Together, they gazed at the rolling waves for a few silent moments.

"Remember that summer when your dad caught us buying beer on our shore leave?" Jules smiled with a faraway look in his eyes. "Nine years ago, maybe. We were, what, seventeen? He ripped into us outside the liquor store. The problem is, you're too easy to spot."

Zeb laughed and ruffled his own white-blond hair, cut short over his deeply tanned forehead.

"And then we found the case of beer in my bunk," Zeb

said. "He must have bought it after he sent us back to the boat. That was when we learned to keep legit when everyone is watching. Twisted lessons from George Artino. That beer tasted so sweet."

They lapsed into a comfortable silence. Zeb stared out to a passing sailboat, lost in memories, while Jules flicked pebbles over a nearby log of driftwood.

"I'm sorry about your old man," Jules said at last. He threw a larger stone in a high arc. "He was a tough bugger, rode us hard, but he was good to me. Gave me a job every summer for years, no questions."

"Thanks." Zeb didn't know what to say in reply, but Jules didn't seem to need any more acknowledgement. Zeb was still working through what he felt about his father's recent death. The suddenness of the accident had shocked Zeb and left him filled with unresolved anger toward his father and guilt at the anger. The man was dead—his father, for all his faults, had still raised him. There was sadness, regret, and questions. So many questions. In darker moments, Zeb wondered whether the old bastard had died deliberately to avoid answering them.

"Did he leave you any money? Or did your sister get it all?" Jules grinned. "I wouldn't put it past Krista to wrangle that somehow."

Zeb smiled then sobered.

"He left me the boat. And half the house. I'll get money once the lawyer deals with the sale. Should be in my account at the end of the month. More money than I've ever had in there. My bank will think I organized a jewel heist."

"That much?"

"Nah, the house wasn't worth much. More than I've ever had, though." Zeb put his hands behind his head and lounged lower in the sand.

"I knew we should have been investment bankers," said Jules. "Then your new cash wouldn't be a shock."

"Yeah, you should have thought of that before you skipped all our high school math classes." Zeb kicked sand toward Jules' foot.

"If they hadn't been so boring, I might have stuck around." Jules shrugged. "I know how to count. That's good enough. What are you doing with the money?"

"Krista wants me to buy a condo, put it back into real estate. That's what she's doing."

"She's so responsible," Jules said, rolling his eyes. "What a smart girl."

"I want to find another *troba*," Zeb blurted out. He hadn't meant to say it out loud, hadn't even known he was thinking about the unformed desire of his heart. The stories his late mother had woven into his bedtime dreams had solidified in the wake of his unanswered questions.

"A troba? Like what your dad made us throw back when we were sixteen?" Jules looked intrigued. "You're still sure that was a troba from your mum's stories and not a deformed dolphin?"

"I want to find out." A half-formed idea started to brew in Zeb's mind.

"Cool. How?" Jules sat up and snapped his fingers. "Your dad's boat. You could take it out and..." He paused.

"Yeah. And." Zeb stood up and dusted off the back of his shorts. Sand sprinkled down. "I need to know where to look. I need to find someone who can help me."

CORRIE

Corrie shoved the key in the ignition of the university rental truck. It turned over with a chuffing groan and settled into a loud roar. She checked her rearview mirror—her plastic jugs were still there, good—and backed the big vehicle slowly out of the parking spot. A car honked at her and she braked suddenly.

"You try driving this beast," she muttered then waved off the other car.

The beach was a solid twenty minutes' drive away, far too far to walk. Even if the lab were beside the beach, she would have driven. When the jugs were full, Corrie could barely lift them.

"Drive to the pier," her lab mate Daniel had said without taking his eyes from the microscope. "Park wherever, they're not going to tow you that quickly. Go down to where the boats tie up, and fill your jugs there. Try to avoid the surface layer, hey? Oil from the boats floats."

Corrie pulled beside the curb near the full parking lot. She was pretty sure she wasn't supposed to park there, but her official-looking truck with the university logo would deter nitpickers. Hopefully. She swung out of the truck and picked up her bag, equipment and supplies in one hand and a jug in the other.

"Now what?" she said to herself. "Balance the other one on my head?"

She grasped the big container around the middle and shuffled to the pier. Halfway there, her thermometer fell out of the bag and onto grass.

"Shit, shit, shit," she said then noticed a family walking by with two small children who stared curiously at her. "Shoot, shoot, shoot."

Nothing was broken, so she tucked it carefully into the

10

bag and carried on her trundling way. Happy shouts floated through the warm breeze. The beach was busy today, with locals enjoying the sun and sand, and the pier even more so. Crab fishermen watched their pots, children ran up and down, and couples strolled and gazed at the view of rugged islands, blue ocean, and bluer sky. Corrie squeezed by a huge cluster of tourists speaking loudly in another language.

"Excuse me," she said, but no one heard. She pushed through with her bulky plastic jugs and they eventually shuffled aside.

Corrie hitched the central jug higher in her arms. Sweat dampened her face and trickled down her chest. The sun beat down on her.

"I'm starting to seriously regret my life choices," she said out loud. No one took any notice. "I used to rent jet skis to tourists. It wasn't so bad. At least it was cool in the water. No one told me science was so much grunt work."

That wasn't true, but Corrie was in a grumbling mood. Her father used to make her do plenty of mundane tasks in his chemistry workshop in their backyard shed. He would experiment, often making something burst into flame for her entertainment, and she would help with excitement and awe. Some of her best memories were made in that shed, despite the repetitive tasks he assigned her. But that didn't mean she couldn't complain now.

Except, no one was there to listen. She waddled down the ramp to a floating jetty on the water. Halfway down, she almost lost her balance when a seagull spread its wings and soared away from its perch on a nearby piling. Its yowling cry made her jump again.

Finally, she reached the jetty and dumped her equipment gratefully on the wooden slats. Her equipment bag was full of sampling apparatus, and she pulled out a refractometer to measure salinity. A plastic component fell off in her hands.

"Hopefully that's not important," she muttered then held

the little device up closer. Instructions from Daniel ran through her head. "Oh, wait, that is important. Damn it. Why does Mara get all the good stuff?" Mara, another student in the lab, had taken the best gear for her fieldwork. She was due back tomorrow, which lessened Corrie's annoyance slightly.

Corrie grabbed a roll of tape from the bag and crafted a makeshift hinge for the device, thanking her overprepared self from earlier. She liked having everything neatly accounted for and taken care of, and while that trait sometimes got in the way of life, it came in handy at times like this.

She took a jug, unscrewed the lid, and kneeled over the edge of the jetty. The water had a thin sheen of oil on its surface, and Corrie sighed. So much for pristine sampling. What would she find in this water?

A plopping noise made her look up. A child's wail crescendoed from above her on the pier.

"My ice cream! It fell!" the child wailed. Corrie sighed again. Great, now she'd probably get bovine DNA in her analysis from remnants in the milky ice cream. Was there a point to this sample?

It was all she had access to now, however. Until her supervisor secured more funding for the lab, they were on a budget. Most of the field funds had been spent on Mara's trip, allocated before Corrie had joined the lab. Maybe one day she could go somewhere to collect samples that would be more likely to answer her scientific questions. Until that day, she would do her best at the pier.

She dipped each jug into the water and filled it up, careful to push the mouth of the jug as deep as she could reach. When she pulled them back onto the jetty, her arms and back protested with the strain. Twenty kilograms were twenty too many. Corrie excused herself from going to the gym today. Not that her plans were usually followed when it came to exercise, but it felt good to have a proper excuse.

A few sad-looking anemones clung to the floating dock below her, just within reach. Corrie donned latex gloves and grabbed a pair of scissors and a plastic sampling bag. She plunged her hands into the cold water and carefully snipped a frond off the closest anemone. At the motion, the anemone and its neighbors curled up, preventing Corrie from taking a second sample.

"I guess that will have to do for now," she muttered. "So much for statistical significance."

Now, how would she get back to the truck? One trip or two? Corrie tapped her foot in thought, then slung the equipment bag around her neck and heaved a jug in each hand. She groaned and took a few toddling steps forward.

"Way too much." She noticed a group of tourists staring at her, and she attempted to turn her grimace into a smile. She could do this. She was a strong, capable woman who could handle anything. It wasn't that far.

It was a long, long way. Her fingers were screaming at her by the time she staggered to the truck and placed the jugs on the ground. She dropped the bag by the driver's side and maneuvered the jugs into the back with shaking arms.

"It's fine," she said to herself. "I'll just make this water last for my entire degree. No problem. I'm sure the answer to all scientific questions resides in this forty liters of seawater."

Corrie turned back to the cab. A large dog, its short black hair gleaming in the sun, sniffed her bag with a pointed snout.

"Scat," she said. The dog looked up. Then it lifted its leg and a stream of urine splashed onto the equipment bag, before it turned and trotted away. Corrie cursed and threw the bag in the bed of the truck. This was just not her day.

Corrie stretched out on the couch at home with a sigh of contentment. She shared a house with three other people—Sophie Trip was a grad student in electrical engineering, Koni Kotaro was working on a graphic design diploma, and Adrianna Rhodes was at vet school—but they were out now buying supplies. She expected them back shortly to set up for the party that their household was throwing tonight.

But first, a blog post. It had been almost a week since her last post, and she had worked on some excellent new correlative data since then that cross-analyzed sightings of the Kraken over time. The data clearly showed a centuries-long migration pattern, which corresponded nicely with changes in ocean temperatures over the same period.

She needed to make a few blog-worthy graphs—more colors, add a legend—but it shouldn't take long. It was exactly what she needed after the last two days of reading scientific papers and fieldwork. Ugh, and meeting Jonathan. She dreaded meeting days, when she felt simultaneously energized by new ideas and dispirited by what she didn't already know. But her blog was pure joy.

It was a data-based examination of mythical sea creatures. She was proud of it. Most sites on the topic wallowed in descriptive accounts from folklore. Corrie had a different purpose: to figure out whether there was any truth to the legends. The best way she knew how to do that was scientifically, methodically. Hypothesize, look at the data, draw conclusions. Her unusual take on the subject had earned her a sizeable following of fervent fans, along with the occasional troll post, which she promptly deleted and expelled from her mind. They didn't know. They hadn't seen what she had seen.

Corrie's mind drifted back to that fateful day when she had seen the mermaid. She opened her blog's archive to search for the post in which she described her encounter as a wide-eyed ten-year-old. That sighting was the impetus for her blog. It was even, if she were honest with herself, the driving force behind her studies in biology. She wanted to know more, find another mermaid, prove to herself that she hadn't imagined it. She wanted to slot the mermaid into the genetic trees of life, figure out how they fit with the rest of the planet.

It was a secret beach. I was so certain I was the only one who had ever found it, with the conviction of a child. But perhaps I was right—the mermaid thought it was safe from prying eyes. I crawled through a tiny crevasse in the rock to find the little cove. One year older, and I wouldn't have fit. I know, because I tried the next year.

She wasn't any sort of human that I've seen before, that much I can safely say. Her fin was covered in shiny scales and looked more like fused human legs than a fish tail, although the feet were elongated, and the toes were webbed. The skin on her naked torso was an odd greenish-brown color, and her hair was long and precisely the color of bull kelp. She was lying on the sand, clearly enjoying the sun. I must have gasped, although I don't remember it. When she heard me, she turned her face my way, and I got a good look at her flattened facial features. Her eyes were large, and her ears were only holes. She gazed right at me for one long moment. Then she gave a terrible screech and flopped back into the water. I might have laughed at the clumsiness if it hadn't been a mermaid doing it.

That moment when our eyes met, that was when this blog was born.

Sorry for the soppy post. I thought you guys might be interested in how this got started. Share in the comments below if you have sighted anything yourself. Back to data tomorrow!

Corrie smiled as she read some of the comments on the post. "You're so lucky," gushed one commenter. "Great post, did you include your sighting in the mermaid data you showed last month?" asked another. "Who are you?" asked one. "We should be besties!"

Corrie snorted at that one. There was a very good reason why she was anonymous online. Aside from the social stigma associated with believing in mermaids and their ilk, she had her career to think of. If word got out that she was studying myths on the side, she would be a laughingstock. No one would take her other work seriously, no one would hire her… Her blog was far too detailed and in-depth for her to write it off as a joke.

Corrie sighed. Then she squared her shoulders, adjusted the computer on her lap, and got to work. Those legends weren't going to find themselves.

An hour later, the front door burst open. Corrie slammed her laptop shut and pasted on a smile. Her roommates didn't know about her secret blog project—no one knew—and she intended to keep it that way.

"Corrie! Good, you're here." Sophie—better known as Trip to her friends—sailed through the open door and up the stairs with a paper bag of groceries in each arm. "Have you set up your science jam stuff yet?"

"Not yet."

"Well, come on! People will be here soon." Trip tutted at her. Corrie grinned sheepishly and shoved her laptop under the coffee table. Trip glided to the kitchen, and Adrianna paused to speak to Corrie.

"Hi Corrie," she said. "The store was out of red food coloring, so I only got blue and green. Is that okay?"

"That's Koni's call, not mine. As long as you have the cornstarch," Corrie said.

"You bet."

Koni entered quietly behind Adrianna with cans of beer in

each hand. He smiled at Corrie.

"Hi, Corrie. I hope you are thirsty."

"I hope you're helping me," she said with an answering smile and took a case from him. "Let's go set up—Trip will be looking for someone to order around."

"I heard that," Trip yelled from the kitchen. "But since you're offering, set up the speakers, will you?"

Corrie followed Koni to the corner of the room, where a large but beat-up speaker system leaned against a bookshelf. Adrianna had found it behind a nearby apartment building, and Trip had tinkered with it to make the speakers play again.

"Set the big one on its back on the coffee table," Corrie directed. Koni complied, and Corrie placed a piece of foil on top of the speaker.

"I still don't understand what this will do," he said. Corrie grinned.

"You'll see. When we play music through the speaker, the foil will vibrate. When we put the cornstarch mixture on it, well, a mixture of cornstarch and water has strange properties, where it can be classified as a solid or a liquid depending on the force exerted on it." She caught Koni's confused expression. "It's going to jump around and look really cool. I'll leave you in charge of the color scheme, okay?"

"I can do that," he said.

Corrie moved to the kitchen, where Trip and Adrianna were arguing about what drinks to put where. They were friends from their undergraduate degrees in university and were tight despite their differences. Trip had grown up on the coast and was brash and brutally honest. Adrianna was from New Brunswick, on the other side of the country. She was quietly strong-willed where Trip was loud, but it was paired with compassion that helped her excel at treating animals. They disagreed often and loudly, but it never appeared to strain their relationship. Corrie and Koni, a Japanese student

17

who had come for his undergraduate degree and had never left, had answered an advertisement for roommates last September. Now, in February, they were all fast friends.

"I hope we have enough vodka." Adrianna looked critically at the bottle in her hand. "If you're going to be lighting half of it up, what will be left to drink?"

"The other half," Corrie said. "And people can blow out the fire whenever they want."

"It's time you had a date, Corrie," Trip said. She took out a mixing bowl and upended a bag of chips into it. "There will be plenty of people here tonight. I want to see mingling and flirting, you hear?"

"All right, all right," Corrie said in defeat. "I'll do my best. But the drinks and science come first. Let me help with the drinks."

"I don't know about you, but I need this party," Adrianna said. "I just got the news that I didn't receive an award I was hoping for, so I have to take more shifts at the vet clinic to pay for tuition." She took out a stack of glasses from the cupboard. "That prissy Laurie probably got it. She's such a suck-up. And annoyingly good at everything."

"Too bad she's so nice, too," Corrie said with a wink at Trip, who laughed. "Makes it hard to outright hate her."

"So annoying," Adrianna agreed.

"Money's tight in my lab, too," Corrie said. "My lab mate Mara used most of it to go on her field season, and now the rest of us are dipping buckets at the beach. My samples are probably total crap. My supervisor is great, but he just doesn't have the money."

"Aren't we all searching for that unicorn," said Trip with a sage nod. "A well-funded, attentive supervisor."

Corrie grabbed a bottle of tequila and clinked it against Adrianna's vodka bottle.

"Hear, hear."

"What do you have planned for the signature drink

18

tonight?" Trip asked. Corrie's mouth curved in a grin.

"I call it the 'fire-breathing narwhal.' Milk on the bottom, blue curacao in the middle, and seventy proof vodka on top. Stick a metal straw in and light the whole thing on fire."

"Sounds insane," said Trip. "And perfect. Are you going to have some yourself, actually live it up for once?"

"Three max," said Corrie lightly, although her stomach knotted at the question. She'd been down the overindulgence road before, and it hadn't ended well. "As always. But you can't say I'm not the life of the party anyway."

"She has a point." Adrianna came to her rescue. "Corrie knows how to party."

"Humph," said Trip. "I guess that's true. I, for one, am going to have one of your ridiculous narwhal drinks, watch whatever crazy show you and Koni came up with, and become better friends with the tequila. And watch you to make sure you flirt, Corrie. Do you hear me?"

"Yes, ma'am."

Corrie grabbed the cornstarch, food coloring, and a few bowls of water and wandered to the living room. Koni was setting up banks of lights in odd places around the room.

"Do you have a plan, or are you winging it?" Corrie asked. Koni looked over from his perch on a chair, where he had hung three different colored bulbs above the door.

"I designed the light effects, and Trip helped me wire it up and program it. You'll see. It will be like magic."

"I believe it," Corrie assured him. He went back to adjusting the lights with a smile. The last party they threw, Trip and Koni had set up jets of glowing water in the backyard, using aquarium pumps and a couple of old barrels, that had pulsed to the beat of the music. It had been a hit.

Corrie kneeled at the coffee table and dripped food coloring into her bowls of water. Trip came bustling into the room with chips. She looked out the window and gasped.

"People are here already!" She checked her watch. "Wow, it's seven. Are you two ready?"

"Close enough," said Koni.

Before Corrie could reply, Trip rounded on her.

"You're not wearing that, I hope."

"What's wrong with it?" Corrie looked down at her outfit. She was wearing jeans—her nicer ones—and a cotton top that was both comfortable and fit well. She preferred comfort to style. Trip rolled her eyes.

"Come on. You look like you're going sampling, not to a party. You have a mission tonight, remember?"

Trip put down her chips and dragged a protesting Corrie toward her bedroom while Koni snickered.

By the time Trip allowed Corrie to emerge from her room, the living room had a dozen guests already clutching drinks and lounging on armrests. Corrie smoothed the front of her skirt in a futile attempt to reduce the fabric's glimmer. Trip had crowed when she had found the skirt stashed behind her lower-key skirts and dresses, left over from her ill-fated undergraduate degree in Vancouver. Corrie had kept it because it was too pretty to give up, made of a shimmery turquoise slinky fabric. She didn't mind showing a bit of skin, but the outlandish material reminded her of wilder times that had led her into trouble.

"Stop fidgeting," said Trip. "You look great." She slapped Corrie on the bottom then pushed her into the living room.

Koni and Trip had worked wonders with the lights. They pulsed with shades of green and blue, shimmering and waving around the room until Corrie felt like she was swimming in the bright Caribbean Sea. She gave a thumbs up to Koni and waded over to him.

"It's amazing," she said. Koni grinned.

"Let's set up the speaker."

Corrie kneeled to finish her task that Trip had interrupted. Green and blue coloring, water, and enough cornstarch mixed together to make a viscous goo. She adjusted the foil on top of the speaker and handed Koni the two bowls.

"Drop cornstarch by the spoonful, in whatever proportion you like. Play with it."

Koni took the bowls from her with a solemn nod, and Corrie wandered to the kitchen. Adrianna and her boyfriend Patrick were mixing drinks, along with a man Corrie had never met. He was about her age, maybe a little younger, with sandy blond hair long enough to show its wavy thickness but short enough to be professional. In a room full of jeans and graphic T-shirts, he stood out in slacks and a buttoned shirt, open at the collar. His face was wide and pleasant, and he turned it to Corrie as she entered.

"Corrie," Adrianna said. "This is David, a friend of Pat's. Get him to help you with your special drinks, will you?"

Corrie gave her a dirty look, and Adrianna unsuccessfully hid her smile. She was on Trip's side, of course, in making sure Corrie mingled successfully. Corrie would be more annoyed if their meddling wasn't coming from a good place. Corrie turned to David and waved him over to the vodka.

"Hi, David. We're going to make a fire-breathing narwhal."

His brow wrinkled in polite confusion.

"I haven't heard of that drink before."

"Because I just invented it." She smiled at him with mischief. If Trip and Adrianna wanted her to flirt, well, never let it be said that she had failed a mission. "It's going to light up your night."

A chorus of cheers broke out when Corrie and David brought out two trays of blue and white drinks, burning brightly with their ephemeral flames. Corrie passed them around, then nabbed two drinks and made a beeline for

21

David.

"Here," she said, passing him a drink. "Try it and tell me how bad it tastes."

David took a sip and grimaced.

"Umm, it's great?"

Corrie let out a peal of laughter.

"I made it for the effect first and foremost. I won't be offended if you don't like it." She took a sip and swished it around in her mouth. "Not bad. But then, I like blue curacao." A fuzzy memory of a violently blue drink backlit by a strobe light flashed through her mind, and she took a tiny sip of her drink to make it last. Three drinks were enough to loosen up, but not enough to reach a level of intoxication that she'd regret. She eyed David up and down and was pleased to see him look agreeably uncomfortable at her once-over. "So, David, what do you do when you're not making flaming drinks?"

"I'm in the last year of my accounting degree," he said with animation. "I'm looking at the big firms for my next step. It's exciting times. Finally, out of school and into a proper job, making real money, on track for advancement. I'm more than ready for it."

Not my life at all, thought Corrie. But Trip would say he's a good catch. David continued to wax poetic about the courses he was taking and tax season approaching. A part of her yawned violently at his description of corporate finances, but a larger part was attracted to him. He was easy to look at, with large hazel eyes and pleasingly broad shoulders. Corrie pondered her attraction while he talked. Was it looks alone? Was it an attraction of opposites, his stable, even-keeled life compared to her unknown future in science? She didn't know, and the jumping balls of green and blue cornstarch on the speaker held no answers.

"What are your plans for next Tuesday?" David asked her. Corrie pursed her lips in thought.

"Clean my fish tank." She waved to indicate she was joking. "Why, what's up?"

"Do you want to go out for coffee with me?"

Corrie looked at him in pleasant surprise. It had been a while since anyone had asked her out on a date. A vision of her ex-boyfriend Dylan snaked through her mind, but she banished him from her thoughts. He was no longer in control—she wouldn't let him be, not anymore, not even in her mind. She gave David a wide smile.

"Absolutely."

ZEBALLOS

Zeb threw a soapy sponge into a bucket of water and wiped his brow with his sleeve. It had been far too long since anyone had given his father's boat a good scrub. While it felt unnecessary, given that he had no plans to take the boat out, washing it gave Zeb something to do with his hands. It was hard enough work that he could avoid thinking, as well.

A thump on the deck made him whirl around. Jules grinned at him.

"You can't make a silk purse out of a sow's ear, my friend," Jules said when he saw the bucket of suds. Zeb shrugged.

"But I can have a clean pig. What's up?"

"You still want to find a troba?" Jules shoved his phone at Zeb, who wiped wet hands on his jeans and took the phone with a raised eyebrow. "Then we need the author of this blog."

Zeb scanned the webpage. Its simple template was filled with articles. Paragraphs upon paragraphs of written material, illustrations, even charts and figures populated the pages. Unquestionably, the author had poured a lot of time and knowledge into the articles, all of which were on the topic of...

"Legendary sea creatures," said Jules. He nodded vigorously. "Perfect, right? She'll have answers, if anybody does. She really knows her stuff. Theories about evolution, DNA, I didn't understand half of it."

"Wait, she?" Zeb went to the About page, which had nothing but a large question mark. "How do you figure?"

"I may not know much about DNA, but I can internet-stalk with the best of them." Jules looked pleased with himself.

"Yeah, I know how much you know about Carole." Jules'

ex-girlfriend posted copious pictures of her life, her cat, and her new boyfriend, and Zeb knew Jules looked at her feeds far too often. Jules scowled but ignored the comment.

"The DNS registration for her website isn't private, so I found out her city and a phone number for a department at the university in Victoria. That narrowed it down somewhat. Then, I looked at a few likely candidates and found some writing samples, journal articles and websites, mainly. One was an Honors thesis, and the style of the writing and graphs was eerily like the blog. But what really tipped me off was the dedication: 'For the legends that inspired me.'" Jules lifted his hands in triumph. "We've got our girl. Basically, I'm a wizard."

Zeb bowed with outstretched arms.

"All hail his magnificence." Zeb looked at Jules expectantly. "Well, who is she?"

"Her name is Corrie Duval. She's a graduate student. She studies bacteria and cancer, or something, which apparently means she needs to sample seawater and anemones along the BC coast." Jules hopped on a container and leaned back.

"How do we get her to help us?"

"Don't worry." Jules grinned at Zeb. "I have a cunning plan."

CORRIE

Corrie stared at the filtration contraption. Seawater dripped slowly into the receptacle. A vacuum pump that sucked air out of the flask to speed up filtration whirred with a noisy roar that grated on Corrie's ears. She wondered if she should bother filtering this water. Would it show anything? Certainly, it was unlikely to contain much, unless she could convince her supervisor that she had discovered the elusive sea cow from the ice cream dropped in the ocean near her. It aggravated her to have contamination like that, as if the seawater itself were out of line.

Corrie sighed and grabbed a beaker to pour more water into the funnel.

"Ah, Corrie." Her supervisor walked past Mara's bench to stop beside Corrie. "I'm glad I caught you."

"Hi, Jonathan." Corrie tried to inject some brightness into her voice, but it still sounded flat and a touch morose. She sat up straighter.

"You went sampling last week?" asked Jonathan. At Corrie's nod, he said, "How did it go?"

"Pretty good." Corrie smiled brightly. It was funny how easy lying came to her boss. She had only been here a few months—she was still aiming to impress. "I got the water fine, and I tried to collect under the oily surface layer. But, I'm a little worried about contamination. What is the quality of my water? There's so much human traffic." *Not to mention errant dairy products*, she added silently.

"Well, we can think of how to test for contaminants, and you can sample somewhere other than the pier." Jonathan sighed and leaned against the lab bench with his arms crossed. "Until I hear about the grant results in a couple of months, I won't know if we have funding for more extensive sampling efforts. However, I received an email from the dean this morning. There's a new award that just came through the pipeline—you should certainly apply. One student from the ocean science program will get a week of ship time, anywhere on the BC coast, all expenses paid. It's on an old fishing vessel, but the lab space looks adequate, I saw pictures. I read the award through, and everything looks on the level."

"Wow," Corrie breathed. She'd never heard of such a generous award before. "Do I have the qualifications?"

"You only have to be an ocean science student at the university. I've emailed you the application. Make sure you submit it, it's due Friday."

"Absolutely. I'll do it right away." Corrie's eye caught her rapidly draining filter funnel, and she scrambled to pour in more seawater. Jonathan pushed off the lab bench.

"I won't keep you."

"Who is funding the award?" Corrie asked. Jonathan paused and turned.

"Some rich kid with an inheritance, according to the grapevine. Apparently loves science, wants to contribute." Jonathan's tone indicated clearly what he thought of the rich kid who loved science without schooling, and Corrie suppressed an eyeroll with difficulty at her boss' snobbishness. "It's an opportunity that you shouldn't let pass you by. Even if the funding for the lab comes through, I could never afford to send you on a solo cruise like this."

"I'll send the application in today," Corrie said, and Jonathan walked out of the lab. Corrie poured more water into the funnel with trembling fingers. Could she win this award? An opportunity like this would be game-changing. She fantasized for a moment, her mind's eye filled with ground-breaking scientific papers authored by her, shaking hands with the dean, naming a new species, *Coralus duvalia*...

There was a dry sucking noise, and Corrie jumped to turn

off the vacuum pump.

ZEBALLOS

Krista stared at her younger half-brother, apparently too appalled for words. Zeb knew they would come, though, sooner rather than later.

"You did what?" Krista finally ground out, her tone usually reserved for expressing her feelings about stepping in dog feces. Zeb had just told his sister about the award, at Krista's apartment during his roundabout way home from Victoria. "And you're only telling me now?"

"I knew you'd act like this," Zeb said, aggrieved and resigned at once. "That's why I didn't tell you until now."

"Damn straight. I would have stopped this harebrained scheme in its infancy." Krista ran a hand through her pixie-cut black hair and sighed dramatically. "I can't believe you would do something so stupid as to contact this sea monster blogger through her university. I supposed Jules put you up to it?"

"It was his idea, but I decided to follow through. It was my decision." Krista already thought Jules was a shiftless slacker with a few bricks short of a load, so Zeb felt bound to defend his friend.

"This is bigger than just you, you realize that, right?" Krista poked him in the chest, then threw up her hands to emphasize her point. "The whole bureaucracy of the university is involved, not to mention the hopes of the student that you'll dash when you withdraw the award."

"I'm not withdrawing anything." Zeb crossed his arms and his chin lifted in a stubborn tilt. Krista's eyes widened in incredulity.

"You can't be serious. Do I have to spell it out for you?"

Zeb said nothing, only tightened his lips. Krista started ticking off points on her fingers with exaggerated motions.

"One. It's a complete waste of money. You're going to

blow Dad's inheritance on a pleasure cruise to hunt for something that doesn't exist. You could be investing that money into real estate, education, hell, even an upgrade on that old beater you call a car. Two. Huge waste of time. You won't have a job if you're out on the boat, and you can't offer diving tours if you have this student on board." Krista started to pace in her agitation. "Then there's the student. Living in such close quarters with a stranger. What if she…" Krista looked at Zeb with a flicker of worry in her eyes. Zeb raised an eyebrow.

"What if she finds out I'm a little different? Come on, Krista. I'm not that careless. I know what to avoid. I've managed to fool everyone so far."

"Jules knows," she snapped.

"Jules is practically family. And besides, I told him, he didn't find out anything on his own. And that's the whole reason for this trip, because I don't really know anything either. I need to know if my mum's stories were real. What that means to me."

Krista's mouth worked, but with nothing to say to Zeb's words, she changed direction.

"This whole award idea is flimsy. And what if this student knows nothing? All you have is some monster-hunting blog to go on. It will be a monumental waste of time."

Zeb waited for a moment. When Krista's tirade appeared to be over, he spoke.

"Are you finished?"

"I covered the basics, yes."

"Thanks for your concern. Just so you know, I'm not entirely clueless. I considered it all before I sent the email to the university. Hell, I even rented a suit and went to a meeting with the Dean of Science. I know you don't understand my reasons, but this is important to me." Zeb sighed and uncrossed his arms. "I'm sure nothing will come of this trip, but I'll regret it if I never try. This student is only around for a week, but hopefully she'll give me a head start. I'll keep looking while the weather's good. At the end of the summer, I'll dock the boat and get a real job. Maybe Tony will hire me back for roofing again. But until September, I'll be on the water. Searching."

Krista scrutinized him for a long moment with her hazel eyes narrowed. Zeb's eyes, that astonishing pale gray, gazed calmly back.

Krista threw up her hands in disgusted defeat.

"You're so stubborn. Whatever, it's your life," she said. Zeb relaxed the tension he hadn't realized his shoulders were carrying. "But you'd better save a berth."

"For who?" Zeb was genuinely puzzled.

"For me, idiot." Krista punched his arm. Zeb rubbed it with a grin he couldn't keep off his face. "Someone has to come along and keep an eye on you. At least while the student is on board. Keep you from doing anything more stupid than you're already doing."

"Jules is coming too," Zeb said.

"Oh, great, dumb and dumber. This will be a riot."

CORRIE

Corrie sat down at her lab bench with a grateful sigh and pulled her laptop toward her. She had a few minutes between experiments to kill—perfect time to check her email. She had been obsessively checking since Friday, when she had submitted her application for the new award. Surely, they had to decide soon. Summer was fast approaching.

The telltale icon of an envelope sent her fingers tapping the mail app. There was junk mail from a laboratory supply chain, a chatty email from her mother, and one from the Department of Biology.

Corrie's heart pounded. Was it a *Dear John, sorry to inform you*, or was it good news? For one frozen moment, she was too frightened to move. Before she checked, both outcomes were possible. When she opened the email, only one would be true.

"Stop dithering," she whispered to herself, and jabbed at the screen with a resolute finger. The email popped open.

Dear Ms. Duval,

We are pleased to inform you that you have been selected for the George Artino award. This is a tremendous honor. The benefactor and captain of the boat would like to meet you early next week to discuss logistics. Please comport yourself as a representative of this university. Best wishes for a successful field season.

There was contact information below for the rich kid, Zeballos Artino, an email address and a phone number. Corrie's hands began to tremble. She had won. Of all the students in the department, she had been chosen for all-expenses-paid week of fieldwork. It was more exciting than the lottery, and it was hers.

"Daniel!" Corrie burst out to her lab mate, who was pipetting stock solutions at a nearby lab bench. "Guess what?

I won that award for the ship time!"

"Really?" Daniel raised his eyebrows and looked impressed. "Congratulations."

"Thanks. I'm beyond excited." Corrie's mind raced through the implications. "This could open up everything. Think of the remote locations I could access, the transects I could sample. This can make my work truly competitive, get publications in the really great journals, open the doors for the best labs for my doctorate…" Corrie stared with awestruck eyes into the distance without seeing anything. Daniel laughed.

"Easy, there. There's a long road between ship time and publication. You need to collect some data first." Daniel finished his pipetting and stripped off his gloves. "Since my projects have no need for fieldwork and I didn't apply for the award, I can see clearly. Don't you think the whole thing is a bit sketchy? I mean, this rich kid who loves science, the old fishing boat turned into a floating lab—you have to admit, it's kind of weird."

"The university checked it out, so it must be okay," Corrie said. She tried not to sound defensive, but it was difficult.

"Yeah, it must be legit." Daniel shrugged and walked over to Corrie. "Who is this guy, anyway? Let's look him up."

Corrie turned to her computer and searched for Zeballos Artino.

"What kind of a name is that?" Daniel asked.

"Strange huh? I think his last name is Greek, but I have no idea about the first name. I wonder if his parents gave it to him, or if he chose it himself." Corrie scrolled down the search results. There wasn't a lot. A Facebook profile and a listing from a high school in a small town on Vancouver Island came up. The rest of the results showed only "Artino" or "Zeballos" separately.

"Zeballos is a tiny village on the western side of Vancouver Island," Corrie said. "And here I thought it was made up by his hippie parents."

"Check the Facebook profile," Daniel said.

She clicked through and they leaned in for a closer look. Most of the profile was private, so all they could see was his name and a sun-flared fuzzy picture of a young man holding up a can of beer. The picture was indistinct and gave no sense of his features beyond a glint of white-blond hair. Corrie leaned back in her chair in disappointment.

"That was a dead end."

"He keeps a low profile," said Daniel. "There's nothing that screams rich kid, but nothing that doesn't, either. Guess you'll just have to meet him and find out. It's not only you and him, is it?"

"There will be a small crew," Corrie said.

"Good." Daniel pushed off from the bench. "Keep us updated while you're out there, so we can sample vicariously through you."

Corrie grinned as Daniel walked away, but she turned his words over in her mind. Should she be more concerned about this award? Was it too good to be true?

No, she decided. It was an amazing opportunity, and she was going to take it and squeeze every last bit of use out of it. She wasn't going to look in the mouth of this gift horse.

Corrie arrived on her bicycle at the marina and locked it up at a railing beside an administrative building. It had been a long ride, but it was one of the first truly beautiful days they'd had this spring, and she hadn't wanted to waste it. A ramp led down directly from the half-full parking lot to a dock that spanned the shoreline and branched off into six perpendicular docks. There were high-speed motorboats, dilapidated sailboats, tiny rowboats, and even a few small commercial fishboats. Metal clinked against metal, and the salt smell of the air made Corrie breathe deeply.

Zeballos Artino had invited her via email to examine the boat for appropriate lab space and to discuss plans. He seemed friendly enough over email, although not forthcoming with details. Corrie was curious to see what he was like in person.

She took off her helmet and wrinkled her nose at her flat hair. She pulled it back in a serviceable ponytail and strode to the dock. Her benefactor had said his boat was on dock five. The floating wooden slats shuddered and gave way underfoot as she wandered down the rows.

At the end of the dock, there was an old fishing boat. Its blue hull was rusted in wear patterns at the bow, although it looked freshly washed. The aluminum cabin was far forward on the boat, leaving plenty of room on the aft deck for winches and other fishing equipment. White curtains were drawn across rounded windows that surrounded a bright orange life ring strapped to the side. It was nothing like the vessel Mara had traveled on, with a crew of twenty-four and berths for twelve scientists. Nevertheless, it was hers to command for the week. The thought thrilled her from scalp to toes.

Corrie wondered how to announce herself and settled on a sharp rap on the metal hull.

"Coming!" a man's voice answered from the interior. Corrie waited with impatience, curious to see the face behind her incredible opportunity.

Short blond hair emerged from the hold first, hair that was so blond it was one shade away from white. It was followed by a good-looking face of a deep olive, Mediterranean hue. When the man glanced up at her, Corrie was startled by the color of his eyes. They were of a gray so pale that only the dark outline of iris prevented the color from bleeding seamlessly into white sclera. The young man pulled himself effortlessly out of the hold and stepped toward Corrie with an outstretched hand. She shook it and noted his firm handshake and warm, dry skin against hers.

"Hi," he said. "I'm Zeb. You must be Corrie. Welcome aboard the *Clicker*."

He helped her step over the bulwark and onto the aft deck.

"Thanks," said Corrie. "Hi. So, this is your boat. Wow, um—" She laughed at her own stumbling. "Sorry, I meant to say first, thank you so much for this opportunity. It means the world to me. You have no idea—my own scientific cruise? Everyone was slack-jawed at the lab. It's amazing. Funding is hard to come by, you know? Everyone likes the idea of science but getting money put toward it is sometimes like pulling teeth. Especially stuff that's not super applicable." Corrie caught herself. "Sorry, I'm rabbiting on. Just, thanks."

Zeb's serious face twitched with a hint of a smile.

"No worries. I came into money recently—Dad died and left me an inheritance—and I wanted to contribute to ocean science somehow."

Corrie glanced him over. He was wearing ripped jeans and a plaid shirt, common apparel for a rich hipster pretending to dress like the working man. To Corrie's eye, however, the holes in the jeans looked worn through rather than artfully ripped. Perhaps he had them pre-worn by someone else for an authentic look. The thought made her smile. Zeb looked at her with a curious tilt to his head and she deflected.

"That's really great of you. Most wouldn't bother. Know that you're helping science and making this grad student's dreams come true." Corrie looked around. "Is there space for lab equipment? I don't need a lot of room, but I do need some."

"Of course, right through here." Zeb led her into the cabin from the aft deck. They entered a narrow space. A short bench was against one wall, and a counter on the other side ran underneath a small window with rounded corners. "Is this

36

enough? We can figure out more space if you need."

"No, this is great. Is there somewhere I can store stuff? I'll need to bring a few jugs of purified water, plus my dive gear."

"Storage space, we have plenty of." Zeb gestured to the aft deck. "The hold is mostly empty. You can fill it up. Anything else you need?"

"I have my own equipment. Oh, but I'll need crushed ice occasionally."

"We have a freezer," he said. "Will ice cube trays and a hammer work?"

"That'll do the trick." Corrie beamed at him. His solution reminded her of MacGyvering solutions to science problems in her father's shed. At home, they had what they had, and she had often helped her father find passable replacements for items they needed for an experiment.

"One more thing," she said. "You don't have an old tank for holding water, do you? It's for my own project that my supervisor doesn't know about, so I can't take one from the lab. If not, no big deal, I'll look on used sites online."

Zeb's eyes gleamed at this, but he said only, "I'll take care of it, don't worry."

"Well, great," Corrie said. She looked around the little room and tried to imagine this boat as her home for a week. It was both bizarre and exhilarating. "Who else is coming?"

"I have two deckhands, Jules and Krista. They'll be helping out with anything you need."

Corrie nodded. A thread of relief snaked through her. As normal as Zeb seemed, spending the week alone on a boat with a relative stranger was a nerve-wracking proposition. Knowing that there would be others, including another woman, relaxed Corrie.

"Why don't you send me a rough plan for the first few days—where you want to go first, how long you need there—and I'll plot a course given the tides and currents. When do you want to go?"

"When can we go?"

"You're calling the shots." Zeb said. "You tell me."

"Soon, I guess. This is crazy. I can really use the boat to go whenever, wherever, for a whole week?" Corrie's heart raced from excitement. It was starting to feel real.

"You betcha. The *Clicker* is all yours."

Corrie slipped her hand into David's, and he gripped it firmly. They were walking down a sidewalk toward the movie theater. David had a movie in mind, but he wouldn't tell her what it was. Corrie could have figured it out by looking at the start times, but she liked surprises. It was sweet of David. They'd been dating for about a couple of months, and she liked how he tried hard to keep things interesting. She would far prefer to try rock climbing or paintball for a date instead of a stereotypical movie, but at least he was trying. They'd gone ziplining last weekend, and while David had gamely gone along and forced a smile when she asked him if he liked it, Corrie could tell he was itching to put his feet on the ground.

But he was sweet, and kind, and they worked well together. He was conservative in bed, but, as always, willing to try to please her. Corrie hoped that the movie wasn't too long. David's place was only a few blocks away, and she intended to take him there straight after. She bumped her shoulder with his playfully.

"You really won't tell me?"

"That's the whole point of a surprise," David said with a sidelong look down at her.

"I guess. I'll just have to talk about something else, then." Corrie thought for a moment. "Oh, remember my sampling trip award?"

"How could I forget?" He smiled to show he was teasing. "You haven't spoke of much else since you found out you won."

Corrie nudged him again.

"Don't be mean. I went to check out the boat yesterday. It's an old fishing vessel, but they use it for chartered diving trips now, so it's kitted out. Bunks are spartan, but they'll do just fine. The lab space is small but more than enough for just me. I think it's going to be great."

"What are the dates again?"

"May first to eighth."

David's face fell, although he tried to cover it up.

"You'll miss our Wednesday night date." He gave her a mock-pout, although she could see it truly bothered him. She sighed inwardly. He was very regimented, and they'd gone out every Wednesday since they started dating. Sometimes she thought it was a sweet ritual, but other times it felt constricting. Mostly, it was sweet.

"I know. But only one. Then we could do something extra special when I'm back."

"Yes. For sure." Corrie could almost see the cogs in David's mind working away at a suitable "something special." Then he shook himself and said, "What about the crew? Did you meet anyone?"

"There will be four of us. I only met the captain. It's the same guy who set up the award, Zeballos Artino. He seemed nice enough."

"Young or old? Model or walrus? Doofus or creepy vibe?"

Corrie laughed, but it was a second before David joined her. Were his questions in earnest? She decided to answer them just in case.

"Close to my age, as far as I can tell." She chuckled again. "Not a walrus. What does that even mean? And like I said, he seems nice. Not a doofus or creepy. I'm sure it will all work out."

"Hmm," David said in a neutral tone. "I'm sure it will, too. Let's plan our special Wednesday date before you go, though, so you have something to look forward to."

"I'd like that," Corrie said. She squeezed David's hand. Was he jealous, or was she reading too much into his questions? She supposed they hadn't been dating long. Although she thought her actions were clear that she liked him, it was still early days. She resolved to show him after the movie that he had nothing to worry about.

"Here we are," David said a minute later. They joined a line to buy tickets for the movie. Corrie looked at the posters and hoped that they were going to *Footprints*, a monster movie that had received good reviews. It was definitely up her alley. They reached the counter.

"Two tickets to *Fall in Love this Autumn*, please," David said to the ticket agent. Corrie's shoulders slumped in dismay. A cheesy chick flick? Was there anything more cliché on date night? At least rom coms were usually short.

"Surprised?" David said as they walked into the theater. "I didn't think you'd expect me to take you to something like this."

"Yeah," Corrie said with an attempt at a smile. "Big time. Are you showing me your willingness to do what I like at your expense?"

"It sounds pretty noble when you put it like that. I kind of like rom coms, though." David put his finger to his lips. "Don't tell anyone."

"My lips are sealed." Corrie pulled David to the back row. If she was going to sit through this movie, she might as well enjoy it. "Come on, be a teenager with me."

Adrianna stood in front of Corrie's closet door, looking at her clothes with a critical eye.

"You'll be gone a whole week on this cruise?" she asked.

"Yep, back next Sunday," Corrie said. "My lab equipment is packed, and now I need clothes and personal stuff." She rolled up the power cord for her laptop and slid it in a backpack. Adrianna let out a deep sigh.

"I don't know, Cor. You're not giving me a lot to work with here. There's still time to go shopping—the mall doesn't close until nine tonight."

"Shopping for what?" Corrie joined Adrianna in her examination of the closet. She leaned forward and slipped three T-shirts off their hangers. "Look at that. I just packed enough for three days. Easy peasy."

"You're hopeless." Adrianna took a black miniskirt off a hanger and passed it to Corrie. "Come on, work with me."

"You do know what I'm doing, right?"

"You're going on a cruise," Adrianna said. Corrie laughed.

"Trust me, it's not that kind of cruise. It'll be a dirty, sweaty, long hours, lab work kind of cruise. Not dancing, drinking, and swimming."

"Oh." Adrianna deflated, then stood straight again. "But you should be prepared for anything. And there's no reason not to look your best even if you're working. If you must wear jeans, make them your cute ones. And take that skirt. What if you go on land for dinner one night?"

"That is unlikely, bordering on impossible."

"Take it."

Corrie took the brandished skirt and accompanying slinky shirt with misgiving. There wasn't much room on a boat in the first place. The only redeeming feature of the skirt was that it was very small.

"Can you take care of my fish when I'm gone?" she

41

asked.

"Of course. Hot Lips is going to miss you." Adrianna cooed at a pleco fish attached to the fish tank's glass with its sucker-like mouth. "Aren't you, Hot Lips?" She pretended to speak like a fish. "Don't go cheating on me with other fish. There may be plenty of fish in the sea, but I'm your best fish."

"Don't worry, Hot Lips." Corrie squished her bag closed and zipped it up. "I'll be studying bacteria and anemones, not fish."

ZEBALLOS

Zeb surveyed his apartment with resignation. His normally sparse studio suite was piled high with boxes of stuff from his father's house. He didn't want it, none of it, but he had to go through every box just in case. Most of it was garbage, but what if there were something of his mother's squirreled away? He had to search through everything to make sure. It would be just like his father to have something that he had never shown his son.

He didn't have time today, though. The sun had set, and he still had to pack for an early morning. The boat was already docked in Victoria, but he and Jules were driving down first thing and setting up for their departure the day after. Jules had his grocery list ready to stock the cupboards, so they had to stop at the store as well.

Zeb found a duffel bag in his hall cupboard and went to his closet to throw clothes inside the duffel. It didn't take long—he packed exactly what he always did for a diving charter, jeans and shirts and a swim suit—and he threw the duffel at the front door with relief.

His gaze caught the items on top of his dresser. Although his furniture was sparse, his collection of treasures was expansive. Most flat surfaces, including the dresser, were covered with shells, dried seaweed, old fishing lures, and other items that Zeb had collected on his many dives. Prominent on the dresser was a plain wooden picture frame with a photo of Zeb as a six-year-old child being hugged by his mother and father.

The picture drew out conflicting emotions in Zeb. There was the usual dull ache when he looked at his mother, as pale as a china doll with hair the color of his own. The picture of his father, his Mediterranean features filled with happiness in a way that Zeb could hardly remember, stirred up a mixture of anger and sadness that Zeb didn't know how to deal with. He moved his eyes to avoid the confusion and spotted his whistle beside the frame.

He nodded decisively. He couldn't forget his whistle. Now that his father was gone, there was no one to stop him playing on the boat if he felt like it. He scooped it up and tucked it into the duffel bag with grim satisfaction.

"Just try to stop me," he said to the photo of his father.

Zeb hadn't closed the curtains of his window yet, and the moon peeked in. Between buildings, the ocean glittered with moonlight. Zeb gazed at it with indecision. He should go to bed soon. It was late.

But a swim would feel so good right now. It took only two minutes to walk to the water's edge from his place. He could swim to his favorite haunts and still be back in an hour, if he left now.

The door closed behind him a minute later.

CORRIE

Corrie woke early, with the sun peeking through her closed blinds. Why was she awake already? A tingling of fear and excitement in her stomach reminded her before her brain did.

Today was the day she would go to sea.

She leaped out of bed and dashed to her closet.

An hour later saw her driving the department truck with a yawning Daniel beside her and equipment in the back. She pulled into the marina's parking lot, found a rolling cart, and started to load her equipment in.

"What if I've forgotten something?" she said when Daniel joined her.

"Relax." He carefully placed a large plastic container on the top of the cart. "You're in charge. Just tell the captain to turn around and come get it. This is your party." He wiggled his fingers for the truck keys. "Good luck."

When Daniel drove away, Corrie gazed after the truck, feeling a little lost. Then she took a deep breath and grabbed the cart's handle with a firm grip.

"This is my party," she whispered. "Let's do this."

The marina was quiet in the early morning. Metal shackles clanked against the masts of sailboats, the sound a gentle beat to punctuate the wail of a seagull in the distance. The thumping rumble of Corrie's cart sang along.

At the end of dock five, voices carried in the still air. Corrie slowed beside the *Clicker* until Zeb popped his head out.

"Corrie! Morning." He leaped over the bulwark with practiced ease and took a plastic container off the top of the cart. He yelled toward the boat. "Jules! Come give me a hand."

Another young man, about Zeb's age, climbed out of the

hold and wiped his hands on a greasy rag. His blue eyes lighted on her. He shook shaggy hair out of his face.

"So, this is our resident scientist." He looked her over. "I always picture scientists with glasses and crazy hair."

"And I always picture deckhands with gray beards and tiny pipes," she shot back. "Looks like we're both disappointed."

Zeb snorted but tried to smother it. Jules grinned.

"I don't bring my pipe out on the first day."

"Jules!"

A tall, lithe woman with Zeb's olive complexion topped with short black hair came out of the cabin and swatted Jules' head hard enough to make him wince.

"Ow, Krista."

Krista glared at Jules, then hopped over the bulwark to shake hands with Corrie.

"Hi, Corrie. I'm Krista, and I'm here to keep these idiots in line."

Corrie grinned and shook Krista's hand.

"Thanks, Krista." She leaned forward and mock-whispered loud enough for Jules to hear. "But between us, he doesn't look too intimidating."

Jules grinned, and even Krista's stern face hinted at amusement.

"Come on," Zeb said. "Let's get packed away. The dive shop delivered the tanks already. I want to be on the water by nine."

He passed Jules a box and Krista jumped aboard again. Corrie and Zeb passed all the equipment to the others until the cart was empty. Before Corrie could climb aboard, Zeb stopped her.

"I want you to know," he said, his mouth stumbling over the right words. "We'll take good care of you and do our best to do what you need for your science."

"Thanks, Zeb." His words helped to reduce the knot in her

stomach. She waved at the boat. "Shall we?"

The others banged around and shouted instructions at each other while Corrie set up her makeshift lab. Her pump, her microscope, even her beakers all had to be secured with an elaborate array of bungee cords and duct tape. She handed scuba tanks and the jugs filled with purified water to Jules in the hold, where the smell of fish was faint but unmistakable. She noted with pleasure a large fish tank strapped down in a corner.

Corrie was sticking a few final pieces of duct tape over an electrical cord when Krista came into the lab. She said nothing but merely looked over Corrie's set-up.

"That should be secured better," she said finally. She pointed at a filter apparatus. "You never know what the ocean will bring us. The seas can get rough, especially if we leave the inside passage."

She spoke in a calm, detached tone, but Corrie detected an unexpected undercurrent of hostility. Had she offended Krista already, somehow? Corrie shrugged inwardly. Hopefully Krista got over it, otherwise it would be a long week. Corrie couldn't change it, so she decided to ignore it.

"Thanks. I'll fix it," she said shortly but politely.

"You're kind of—" Krista coughed and obviously rephrased what she was about to say. "Super organized, hey?"

Corrie looked at her color-coded lab tape and carefully hung tubing in order of size. Yes, she was particular, but it only helped in the lab. She weighed giving a sharp answer back but decided against it. Krista said nothing further and moved out to the aft deck.

Zeb came into the lab while she admired her secure filter apparatus.

"How are you doing? Just about ready to go?" he said, a vein of excitement in his voice.

"Ready when you are." Her voice was steady, but inside

47

her mind whirled with everything she needed for her first station.

"Come up to the wheelhouse, if you like," Zeb said. "It's the best view forward. And the warmest spot, you'll find."

"But it's such a nice day," Corrie said as she followed Zeb forward.

"I hope you brought a sweater, because it's always colder on the water."

They entered the wheelhouse, which was a cozy narrow space with windows on the front and bookshelves and a counter on the back. A door on the starboard side was clipped in an open position, and one high chair swiveled in front of a large wooden wheel. The wheel reached to Corrie's shoulders, and its turned wooden handles were polished with age and use to a fine golden sheen. Another seat folded out from the wall.

"Look at that wheel," said Corrie. She stepped up to touch it. "It looks like it should be on a pirate frigate. Argh, matey!"

Zeb smiled.

"My dad wasn't very whimsical, but that wheel is the exception. It was salvaged from some wreck—he never told me where—and it's been on this fishboat as long as he's owned it."

"What was your dad doing with an old fishing boat?" Corrie asked. It didn't jive with what she thought she knew of the "rich kid." Zeb shrugged.

"Eccentric hobby." He waved at the folding chair. "Have a seat. I'll start us up."

Zeb leaned out of the door and yelled the news of their departure. Jules called back, and Zeb started the engine with a grating roar. Krista appeared at the bow to unhitch the headline from the dock. She waved her completion at Zeb then hopped on board and secured the headline to a cleat.

Zeb eased the boat away from the dock with a casual effortlessness that told Corrie he'd done this many times before. The boat slid out the channel between other vessels lined up at moorage until they were out, past the breakwater, out at sea. Corrie felt a tingle of excitement and glanced at Zeb. His eyes crinkled with amusement at her eagerness.

"We're off. You might as well get comfortable, it's a few hours until our first station. Why don't you tell me more about your project? I read your application, but I'd rather hear it from you."

"Oh! Sure." Corrie deliberated for a moment. She still wasn't sure what Zeb's deal was. She hadn't known what to expect, but a down-to-earth, fishboat-driving young man wasn't it. What did he want to know? What would he understand? "I'm looking for plumose anemones, you know, the big white fluffy ones."

"I've done lots of diving," Zeb said. "I know them."

"Oh, right." Corrie paused, a little embarrassed. It was always difficult to judge in how much detail she should discuss her scientific work. "A certain strain of bacteria is commonly found in the fronds of those anemones, and they produce an anti-cancer compound. People are very interested in harvesting that, obviously, or even better, growing the bacteria in the lab and reproducing the compound widely."

"And you're trying to figure out where and how the bacteria grow on the anemones? Different water temperatures, for example?" Zeb said, his eyes raking the sea for other boats. Corrie blinked in surprise at his insight.

"Exactly. If we want to replicate production of the metabolite—sorry, the compound—in the lab, we need to know more about the compound and how the bacteria grow and produce it. That's where my study will contribute needed information. And it's fascinating that these bacteria are producing it in the first place. What drove their evolution to produce it? What do they use it for? What's their relationship with the anemones?" Corrie stopped and flushed. "Sorry, I'm rabbiting on. That was a long-winded answer to what I'm sure was a polite question."

Zeb shook his head.

"No, it's interesting. I wouldn't have invited you on board if I didn't think so."

"That reminds me, what's your story?" Corrie watched Zeb's face, which stilled at the question. He took a moment to answer. When he spoke, it sounded well-rehearsed.

"It doesn't reflect well on me, but okay. I've never taken much seriously, skated along life, relying on handouts from my father." He paused, either struggling with emotion or remembering the right words. "Then, when he died, it was a wakeup call, you know? I wanted to do something more, something with meaning. But I don't have a lot to offer, except money from the inheritance. So, we came up with this idea."

"We?"

"Jules and I go way back."

Corrie turned over this information in her mind.

"I think that's great. Most people wouldn't do that, no matter how much inheritance they got. And I'm sorry about your father."

He cast her a swift, tight smile.

"Thanks. We never really saw eye-to-eye, but it's still strange having him gone. I think Krista's more cut up about it than I am."

"Krista?"

"She's my half-sister."

Corrie looked closer at Zeb's face and nodded slowly.

"I see it now. The hair and eyes threw me off. Can I ask—never mind."

"Go on." Zeb's mouth twitched. "Spit it out."

"Is that your real hair color?"

"Yup. Mum was really pale. And I don't wear colored contacts, either, in case you were wondering. I've had that question before, too."

"It's unusual," Corrie admitted. "But nice. I mean, you look good." At Zeb's questioning glance, she reddened. "Oh, hell. I'm going to check my equipment before I put my other foot in my mouth." She moved to the door.

"Feel free to come back and compliment me anytime," he called after her. Corrie smiled to herself.

JULES

When they arrived at the first station, off the tip of Valdes Island in the Strait of Georgia, Jules had already mastered the swaying walk that enabled him to move around the deck with ease. His dad might run a bookstore, unlike Zeb's fisherman father, but that didn't mean he knew nothing about being at sea. He'd worked on this boat often enough.

In the galley, Jules put the finishing touches on his pantry organization. Space was tight on the boat, but he had storage down to a fine art. He kneeled to reach deep into the lowest cupboard, and his fumbling fingers hit a switch. He peered inside.

Mounted on the back panel of the cupboard was a small light switch. Jules tilted his head in thought. He didn't remember ever seeing that switch, but had he ever sat on the floor and looked? He wondered what it did and flicked it a few times. Nothing happened. Was up or down the off position? He supposed it didn't matter, not if it didn't do anything. He closed the cupboard and headed outside.

Wind pushed Jules' shaggy hair off his forehead, and he took a deep breath of salty, clean air. The crisp coolness reminded him of fresh lemon, and the saline undertones of a just-caught lingcod. He'd have to tell Zeb to schedule in some fishing time if they were to eat anything half-decent this week. Zeb might be fine with throwing some fish sticks in the oven and calling it dinner, but Jules had higher standards.

When Zeb yelled out that they had arrived, and the motors dwindled from a throaty roar to a rumble, Corrie burst through the aft door with her gear. There was a wild gleam in her eye, and her fingers twitched around her clipboard.

"Ready to do some science?" Jules said. Corrie's leg jiggled in anxious anticipation.

"I hope so," she said and opened a container that she had dragged out earlier. Inside was a black bottle with a cap on either end and cords poking out at random intervals.

"If you don't get it right the first time," Jules said. "You have all week to perfect your technique." Corrie looked like she could use some calming down. To his relief, her shoulders relaxed.

"That's true."

Jules lifted the black bottle gingerly.

"What do you want done with this?" he asked, holding it aloft.

"It's called a Niskin bottle, to collect seawater at depth," she explained. "You drop it overboard on a line, and when it's at the depth you want, you send the messenger." She pointed at meter markings on the line then held up a small weight with a clip. "And it triggers the lids of the bottle to close."

"If I'd known, I could have rigged up the winch for you," said Jules. He walked to the edge of the boat. "Next station, we'll have a proper setup. You can always ask. I'm not just a pretty face."

Corrie grinned.

"I'll keep it in mind. For now, let's just throw it over."

They collected water from a few depths. Jules was particularly enamored of a jellyfish that clung to the top of their bottle. When Corrie dropped it in a bucket of seawater, it pulsed in a flowing pattern to the beat of its own music. Jules wondered if he had remembered to pack gelatin in their supplies. He had a sudden hankering for panna cottas.

CORRIE

"Zeb? Get up here!" Krista shouted from the wheelhouse. "There's something weird jumping out of the water."

Corrie and Jules exchanged a look. What had Krista seen? Jules turned to scan the waves.

"There," he pointed. "I saw it too."

"What is it?" Corrie scanned the waves. There was some chop today, and the sea could conceivably hide all manner of secrets in the troughs of its waves.

"A fish, maybe this long." Jules held his hands apart to the length of his forearm. "It was rainbow-colored, like an El Dorado, jumped like a flying fish, and had a growth on its head like a horn. Totally bizarre." He snorted. "The little-known unicorn fish of the Pacific."

Corrie held her breath and scanned the water with more intensity. She needed to see this creature. The ocean was notoriously deceptive, and while part of her wanted to believe Jules at face value, her scientific brain needed evidence. Perhaps it was a flying fish with a deformity, although they weren't usually found in cold waters. And the fish was too small and the waters too cold for an El Dorado, the shimmery dolphin-fish of the tropics. Corrie ran through her knowledge of local fish for a match to Jules' description, but came up with nothing.

"There!" Jules pointed. "There are three of them!"

Corrie's eyes followed Jules' outstretched finger. Three slender fish leaped out of the waves and flapped their tails behind stiff bodies. They were stabilized by short pectoral fins that spread horizontally, their ribbed webbing held rigid. Their bodies glistened in the sun in a hundred glittering colors that changed with every movement. Above each pointed nose was a protrusion, no longer than Corrie's finger, that jutted out at an angle. The composition of the horn was difficult to tell from a distance, but Corrie could make out swirling ridges that spiraled to a translucent tip, as if long fish bones were twisted together.

Corrie's mouth gaped open. This was insane. The three creatures leaping in the distance were like nothing she had ever heard of before. One might be an aberration, a mutant, but three? Had they discovered a new species?

"So?" Jules said. "What does our resident biologist think they are?"

"I don't know," said Corrie faintly. "They look like young salmon, with specialized pectoral fins. And the horn…" What was she supposed to say? They weren't like anything she knew. What did this mean? She had to find out what the fish were. "I'm going to the wheelhouse."

Corrie squeezed past Jules and poked her head into the wheelhouse. Krista continued to helm the boat, with occasional glances at the leaping fish. Zeb looked through a pair of binoculars but fastened his pale gray eyes on Corrie when she entered.

"Well?" Zeb said, his voice strained with his effort to appear unconcerned. "What are they?"

"I don't know." Corrie glanced at Krista, who stared resolutely forward. Was that why Krista was unfriendly to her? Because she guessed Corrie's secret obsession? She looked back to Zeb's guarded eyes. "What if we made a detour to follow the fish?"

Zeb's eyes flashed with excitement, but he glanced down at a chart to hide it. Krista shot him a sharp look. Corrie frowned. What was going on?

"Is that why you needed an aquarium tank on board?" Zeb asked.

Corrie colored, then stuck her chin out.

"In science as in Scouts, one should always be prepared."

"We take directions for sampling from you." Zeb waved at the charts. "We'll follow as long as it's safe. Tell Jules to prepare the dinghy and the nets." He dropped his formal air. "Today, we're hunting rainbow unicorn fish."

ZEBALLOS

Corrie rushed out of the wheelhouse as the boat angled with their change in direction. Zeb heard her shouting for Jules as he followed.

"Jules! We're going to try to catch one. Zeb said to get the dinghy and nets ready."

Jules clapped his hands.

"Right. Fishing is something I can do. Here, help me with the dinghy cover."

Zeb stepped forward to help Jules. Krista kept their course to follow the fish around a small forested island, then the fish dived and didn't resurface.

"Damn it!" Corrie said loudly. "Now what?"

Zeb raced to the wheelhouse and Corrie followed. When she entered, he was pouring over a chart.

"There's a strong current here," he told Krista.

"I see it," she replied. Zeb looked up at the band of darker rippled water ahead of them.

"Take the current north," he said. "They'll likely follow it to the open stretch. Hopefully they'll surface there."

"On it," said Krista. She turned the wheel and the boat tilted. Zeb looked at Corrie. His stomach was clenched in anticipation. Had it really been that easy? Their first day out on the water, and they had found something. Was Corrie a good-luck charm? Had the secrets he'd been wondering about been swimming in the Strait all this time?

Could they catch a fish to find out?

"Let's find you a life jacket. We'll take the dinghy soon, I have a feeling."

Corrie raced away. Krista gave Zeb a dark look.

"Don't get your hopes up," she said. "We're a long way from catching it. And it might just be a deformed rockfish."

Exasperation at Krista's naysaying filled Zeb's chest, but

he said only, "We won't know until we try."

He followed Corrie to the aft deck, where Jules was loading nets and poles into the dinghy.

"What else do you need?" Jules asked.

"I don't know!" Corrie danced on the spot. "Nets? I don't know how to catch a fish. I normally deal with anemones!"

"Chill, Corrie." Jules patted her shoulder. "I only meant if you needed a special piece of equipment. We'll do our best to catch one, okay?"

"Here's a life jacket," Zeb said from behind her. She turned and clutched the orange vest. Zeb pointed past the bow. "There's a kelp bed ahead, a big one. My best guess is they'll make for that. So, let's get the dinghy ready to float."

"There they are!" Jules yelled. Zeb whipped his head around to look. The fish leaped into the air toward the kelp bed, just as he had predicted.

Zeb pulled a walkie-talkie off his belt and spoke into it. His fingers dug into the button.

"Stop the boat, Krista. We're going to launch the dinghy."

"Roger," Krista's voice crackled, and the engine rumbled down to a quiet roar. Zeb waved Jules to the winch control and slid into a life jacket.

"Corrie and I will follow the fish. Winch the dinghy overboard. I'll radio when we're ready for pickup."

"Aye aye, captain." Jules winked at Corrie and pulled a lever. Gears ground and chains clanked as the winch drew up slack. Corrie jiggled with impatience beside Zeb, and although he maintained a stoic calm, inside he was as jittery as Corrie looked. He recalled Corrie's blog, and wondered fleetingly what was going through her mind right now. She must be almost as hopeful as he was.

The dinghy slowly swung over the side and landed in the water with a splash. Zeb climbed over the edge and dropped into the dinghy, then turned to give Corrie a hand. Corrie dropped beside him before he fully extended his arm.

58

"We're on a time constraint," she said. "No time for gallantry, although I appreciate the gesture."

"Noted," he said. "Start the motor while I unhook the chain, then."

"Aye aye," she said. Zeb's face twitched in an involuntary smile.

"Not you, too." When the motor roared to life from Corrie's yank, Zeb took the handle and sat in the stern. "Let's go fishing."

The motor had decent horsepower, and they zipped over the waves at a good clip. Corrie held onto the side with the wind whipping loose strands of her braided hair in her face. Zeb squinted against salt spray and the sun and soon spotted the three fish jumping ahead. A mass of brown fronds, nearly an acre in size, spread in front of them on the surface of the heaving water.

"We won't go through the bull kelp," Zeb yelled over the noise of the motor. "It'll wrap around the propeller. We'll circle around and intercept them."

Corrie gave a thumbs up and grabbed a handheld net from the bottom of the boat. It was nearly as long as she was tall, and Zeb masked a smile as he imagined her trying to wield it.

The fish dived under the edge of the kelp bed and disappeared. Zeb slowed the motor and they chugged around the perimeter. Zeb strained his eyes for any clue as to the fishes' whereabouts. Corrie pointed at a clump of kelp.

"I think that kelp moved," she said.

"Kelp beds are teeming with fish," Zeb replied. "I wouldn't rely on movement to track them. No, we'll go to the other side and try to spot them when they emerge."

"Zeb? Anything?" Krista's voice came through the walkie-talkie.

"They're in the kelp. We'll wait them out for a bit. Over."
"Roger."

The island on their left was heavily forested and

uninhabited, and waves crashed on the rocky shore. Corrie asked about it.

"Valdes Island," Zeb said. "Hardly anyone lives there."

Corrie looked back at the kelp, and Zeb's eyes followed. A distinctive flash of silvery rainbow caught his eye at the edge.

"Damn it!" Corrie yelled. "There they are! They were too quick. Can we cut them off?"

"Too fast," Zeb said, but he gunned the motor anyway and held up the walkie-talkie. "Krista, we're chasing them around the corner. Over."

The fish leaped and soared closer to the island. Zeb's gaze raked over the rocks, where a dark chasm slowly revealed itself. The fish made a beeline straight for it.

"They're going in that cave," Zeb said to Corrie. "Hang over the bow. I need you to watch for rocks."

Corrie's face set in determination, and she shuffled to the bow and draped herself over the metal. The water was murky in the open but clear in the shallows.

"Rock there," Corrie squealed and jabbed her finger at the offending protrusion. Zeb deftly slid the dinghy past without danger.

The cave beckoned with a dark menace. The sides dripped with seawater and barnacles, and although the cave was wide, the roof was low. Beyond the first few boat lengths, all was darkness. Zeb's jaw clenched at the danger to his dinghy, but they were too close to answers. They had to find the fish, find out if it was what Zeb thought it was.

"Do we have a flashlight?" Corrie called out.

"Maybe a flare," he replied. He rustled in the emergency bag behind his feet to extract a flare. He tossed it forward and the flare struck the boat near Corrie's feet. "There you are. Should give us a few minutes. How big can this cave be?"

"Famous last words," she muttered. Louder, she said, "Rock on your right!"

"Starboard," he corrected with a smile in his voice. "You need to learn the lingo on my boat."

Corrie didn't respond to his jibe. The light was growing dim and the blackness ahead was eerie. Corrie reached around with her hand to feel for the flare without taking her eyes off the rapidly darkening rocks below the clear water. She turned for a moment to light the flare with fumbling fingers, and Zeb slowed the boat while she was inattentive to dangers. When Corrie finally struck the flare against the rough surface of the cap and averted her eyes from the dazzling red flame, she held the flare high over her head and gasped.

"What?" Zeb hissed. Then he looked down and let out his breath in a whistle. He put the engine in neutral and let the boat drift in the wide cave.

Strolias swirled everywhere. A whole school drifted in the waters below the dinghy, their colorful scales glinting in the flare's light as they slid their bodies against one another. Their horns were easier to see now—a swirl of translucent fish bones that water could pass through—and for a moment Zeb couldn't breathe. They were just how he had always pictured them, just how his mother had described them.

"Damn it. I forgot my camera!" Corrie's voice came out in a frustrated squeak. "Can you net one?"

"How could I not? They're everywhere." Zeb slid the handheld net toward him and held it over the water. Corrie lifted the flare higher to give him more light, and the fish glinted in the clear water like a bowl filled with rubies.

Zeb braced his knees on the bottom of the dinghy, lifted the net over the water, and stilled. He waited for a breath with his heart thumping painfully in his chest. With a sharp jab down, Zeb plunged the net in and scooped it through the water.

It was pandemonium. The surface exploded with finned bodies. Water sprayed, and tails slapped. Corrie shrieked and the flare wobbled. Zeb struggled with the net as hundreds of fish leaped to the mouth of the cave and the water boiled beneath the hull.

When the water calmed, Zeb held aloft the net. Wriggling and flashing in the red light, a strolia thrashed in the ropes. Zeb hardly blinked for fear he would miss a second of seeing this legend come to life.

"Get the bucket!" he yelled, all dignity forgotten. "Fill it with water. Quick!"

Corrie scrambled to dip a bucket below the boat's edge and strained to lift it into the boat. Zeb carefully guided the net toward the bucket. Corrie moved forward to help, but Zeb shook his head.

"No, stay back. That horn is sharp. Looks sharp," he corrected himself. Also, if his mother's stories were correct, the tip was poisonous. Corrie backed away to the bow, but she watched with wide eyes.

Deftly, Zeb dipped the net into the bucket and wiggled the fish out. It swam in agitated circles, its horn scraping the sides of the bucket every few seconds in an uneven rhythm. They stared at it for a moment.

"We did it," Corrie whispered. She looked at Zeb with shining eyes. "We caught it. A strange new morphology, possibly a whole new species. This is incredible." A little laugh escaped her. "How did we get so lucky so quickly? What do you think we should call it, *Corricus Zeballus*? Unicorn fish to the layman?"

Zeb snorted. Corrie was already thinking of her science career, but he couldn't stop going over all the stories that his mother had told him as a child. What else lurked in the deep? What else might they discover? What else in the stories was real?

"I'll leave the scientific naming to you. Come on, let's get this bad boy to your aquarium tank."

KRISTA

The radio crackled to life. Krista grabbed it.

"We caught one," Zeb said through the static. "Coming back now. Over."

"Roger that," Krista replied. "Over and out."

She replaced the radio in its cradle then looked over to Jules, who lounged with his feet up on the counter. Krista eyed his boots with distaste but simply shook her head. Everything she said to Jules regarding manners tended to slide off his back like he was a particularly oily duck. She'd given up years ago.

Besides, they had more important things to discuss.

"Tell me something honestly, Jules." Krista crossed her arms and faced Jules squarely. He put his hands behind his head and looked at her.

"I always do," he said. "What's eating you?"

"That creature you and Zeb saw on the boat when you were teenagers." Krista couldn't bring herself to call it a troba. That would be giving too much credence to Zeb's mother's stories. "Really, what was it?"

Jules shrugged.

"Dunno. Could have been a mutant porpoise. Weird color, though. And I swear it had gills. Could have been some Frankenstein experiment gone wrong. But, really, Zeb's theory that it's an undiscovered species that his mother somehow knew about, it's as good a theory as any."

Krista released her breath explosively.

"Damn it. I need Zeb to put this to rest. Move on with his life. He's obsessed for months about whatever secrets Dad was keeping from him. It's not healthy. I was expecting this trip to show him that there's nothing else out there, and then he could let it die a natural death. But now? Whatever this unicorn fish is, it's only going to fan the flames."

63

"Yeah, he's not going to stop now that he's getting proof. But don't you think there might be something to the stories?" Jules looked at her with curiosity. "Zeb is different, after all. Is his theory really so far-fetched?"

"Yes, it is," Krista snapped. "Don't go feeding into his obsession." There was something different about Zeb, just like there had been something different about her step-mother, Clicker. But helping Zeb find answers was less important than keeping him safe. Krista had promises to keep, and she never made promises lightly.

ZEBALLOS

Zeb pushed the little dinghy motor as fast as it could handle, and the engine whined. Corrie gazed at the bucket between her feet with rapt attention, her conversation stifled by their discovery. Zeb stole glances when he could. Every so often, the horn of the fish poked out of the top and a shiver ran down his spine. He wanted to look at it more closely. He needed to.

"What will you do first?" Zeb's voice was hoarse with anticipation and tension. Corrie looked overwhelmed at the question.

"Put it in the tank and observe, first. Observations always come first in science. Then, maybe some water samples, try to swab the skin, analyze it for proteins and DNA back at the lab…" She shook her head. "We'll have to play it by ear."

Zeb nodded, but couldn't force any more words out of his tight throat. They approached the boat, and Krista came to the deck to help bring the dinghy up. Her expression was stern and resigned, and Zeb could practically hear her consternation over their capture. He wondered if this would finally make her believe.

He pulled up next to the boat and Krista leaned over the side.

"Here, pass it up first," she said, her hands at the ready to grab the bucket. "I'll send the winch over in a minute for the dinghy."

Corrie took the bucket and carefully stood in the swaying dinghy. She gripped the bucket with both hands, then slowly raised it to Krista's waiting ones.

Before Krista could grasp the handle, a wave hit them broadside. The dinghy rocked, and Corrie wavered. Water in the bucket sloshed. The movement must have frightened the fish, for it made one last attempt at freedom. It leaped out of the bucket, body flipping back and forth, scales winking brightly in the sunlight. Zeb cried out and dived forward to catch it, poisoned horn be damned. He couldn't let it get away. His fingers almost landed on the creature's tail, but his fist grasped only air. The fish flopped over the edge of the dinghy and splashed into the ocean.

"No!" Zeb shouted. He stood and prepared to dive in. Swimming was as simple as breathing for him. If he dived in now, there was a chance he could recapture the fish. It was his first sighting of a strange creature since the troba. He needed to catch it.

"Zeb!" Krista's voice was sharp with a hint of fear. He paused, and the moment to catch the fish died. He balled his fists. He knew that Krista didn't want him to act strangely in front of Corrie, but her hesitance had made him lose the chance to get the fish. It was a strolia from his mother's stories, he was convinced of it. But now he couldn't be certain beyond a shadow of a doubt, because they didn't have the creature on board. Krista couldn't understand the draw the answers had for him. He stayed facing the sea for a moment, breathing hard, too angry to meet his sister's disapproving eye.

"Were you going to jump in after it?" Corrie asked, her voice incredulous. "Better you than me. It's freezing in there."

The cold never bothered Zeb. He imagined the fish sliding through the cool, green water, forever out of reach, and his usual stoic façade cracked. He took a breath then slammed his fist against the hull. It made a dull ringing sound.

"How did we lose it? Hundreds of strolias. We even caught one, and it got away."

He ran his fingers through his short hair, trying to master himself.

"What did you call them?"

Zeb kept his eyes on the sea to avoid Corrie's gaze. He

hadn't meant to let that word slip. They were calling them unicorn fish before; while not original, it was at least descriptive. He was supposed to be getting Corrie to talk about her monster interests, not his. No one else needed to know. Krista and Jules were enough.

"It just came to me." He picked up the net and tossed it to Krista, who glared at him in remonstration for letting the word slip. "Let's get on deck."

"And figure out what the hell those were, and how to catch one?" Corrie said with a question in her voice.

While she was the director of scientific operations on board the *Clicker*, Zeb was still the captain and had the final say for their sampling program. But this was the opportunity he had been hoping for, dreaming for, and the same eagerness infused Corrie's question. Zeb met her eye.

"I was hoping you'd say that."

CORRIE

Corrie climbed out of the dinghy using the ladder that Krista had slung over the side. Her body shook from adrenaline and disappointment. The unicorn fish had been in the bucket. They had been so close to bringing it aboard, examining it, studying it. She dug her nails into her fists in frustration. She'd been hoping for something like this ever since she had seen the mermaid. Something, anything, that would prove that she wasn't making it all up. She didn't know how they could have found something so incredible on their first day at sea. Why didn't everyone know about the unicorn fish if they were that easy to spot?

This was big. So big. Had they discovered a new species, or at least a morphology so different it was worth documenting? Could this change her career, or science itself?

Could they catch one first?

"I had so many tests I wanted to run," she burst out when Zeb cleared the deck, his mouth and eyes grim. Krista had retreated into the cabin. Corrie slammed her fist into her palm. "How could we be so unlucky?"

Zeb shook his head tightly.

"We just need to try again. Come up with a plan." He glared at the ocean in the direction of the cave. "We can set up a net trap in the cave. Fish can be habitual. Or maybe they like caves in general—we find other caves and put traps in their entrances. We could dive to find more. Let's not give up." Zeb's words were hopeful, but his tone held all the disappointment that Corrie felt. He was very enthusiastic about the unicorn fish, even though to him they were surely no more than a weird species of salmon. Although, he had called them by a funny name…

"I'll get a net," Zeb said. "We'll go by the cave on the way to your next station and I'll set up the trap. Let's keep

68

doing your stations but keep an eye out for caves on the way. We can circle back here tomorrow."

Corrie nodded, and Zeb walked toward the wheelhouse. She took one last look at the water, but when no flashes of rainbow shimmered on the surface of the sea, she turned to go to the lab. She had science to do while they waited for their lucky break. Although the unicorn fish wasn't a mermaid, its uniqueness would validate her blog, validate her whole belief in the legendary. This opportunity was too amazing to ignore. However, she had plenty to do in the lab while she waited for a unicorn fish to appear. While not legendary, her work on metabolites was important and far more likely to help her career.

Corrie froze. She might not have a unicorn fish, but she had the water that it swam in. Were there traces of the fish in the water? Urine, scales, any excretions it might have made— Corrie whirled around to find the bucket. It sat forgotten on the deck, half-full of seawater. She carried it carefully to the lab. It was a slim chance, really no chance at all, but if she could concentrate any DNA from this water, she might be able to find something out about the fish.

Corrie stayed in the lab when Zeb ran the dinghy to the cave once more with Jules. She had plenty of samples to prepare and analyze, and she couldn't face the disappointment of the empty waters of the cave. Sure enough, when the dinghy returned, Zeb's face was shuttered, and he went to the wheelhouse without a word. Jules leaned against the lab's doorway.

"No unicorn fish in sight, but the net's all set. When's our next station?"

"A couple of hours, I think," Corrie said. She pursed her lips in concentration as she pipetted a chemical solution into a sample tube. "Niskin bottle, same as last time, but diving as well. I need to collect some anemone samples."

"Roger that," Jules winked at her and gave her a salute.

"We'll be ready. But first, lunch. I'll call you when it's made." He disappeared into the galley and Corrie's shoulders slumped. Then she tightened her jaw. The unicorn fish might be back tomorrow. And when it was, she would be ready.

ZEBALLOS

"I'll drive to the next station," Zeb said shortly to Krista, who was at the wheel. She arched an eyebrow at his brusque manner.

"Whatever. Don't forget to time the narrows right."

"Yeah, I got it." Zeb didn't want to talk. He didn't want to hear his sister's remonstrations, or discuss the disappointment that welled up inside, threatening to choke him. He just wanted to be alone.

Krista seemed to get the hint, for she said nothing else. Her fingers lightly pressed his shoulder, then she was gone. Zeb sighed and slumped over the wheel.

It was unbelievable, really, that he had been so lucky so quickly into his search. To see a whole school of strolias on day one—the odds were incredible. But that didn't negate Zeb's crushing disappointment at the loss of the strolia in the bucket. To be so close to potential answers, and to have them ripped away—it was almost too much to bear. After all, he'd been in and on the water all his life, and he had only ever encountered the troba before, with Jules on his father's boat. Who knew when he might have another encounter with the world of his mother's stories? Had he just squandered the last sighting he would have this decade?

With that dispiriting thought, Zeb peeled himself off the wheel and put the boat into gear. He still had a job to do. He'd promised Corrie a week of sampling, and he would fulfill that promise. He only hoped her interest in the strolias was as keen as his own.

He drove in solitude for an hour, with only his thoughts and the roar of the engine for company. They turned around a large island, and Zeb's watchful eyes spotted a dark patch on the island's rocky shore. His heart leaped. He slowed the boat and grabbed the intercom.

"Krista, wheelhouse."

A minute later, his sister emerged from the doorway. Her mouth twisted in displeasure.

"Don't take your captain duties too far, little brother. I may have tolerated Dad's authoritarian rule, but I won't take rudeness from you."

"But, Krista, look." Zeb pointed at the cave, then said hurriedly, "Sorry. But I need you to take the wheel while I put out a net in that cave."

Krista gazed at him and then sighed. Her face was hard to read.

"Fine. Hurry up, though. Jules wants to serve lunch before we get to the next station."

Zeb tore out of the wheelhouse. He had put the dinghy in so many times by himself that he didn't need help. The winch swung the dinghy over the edge and dropped the little vessel in the water with a splash. Zeb grabbed a net and some tools and vaulted over the edge. With a yank at the motor's pull, he zoomed away.

The cave was small, more so than he had reckoned from the wheelhouse. It wouldn't take much netting to cover the entrance. He had rigged up a crab trap-type entrance in the center of the net. Any strolias that swam through the small opening would be unable to swim back out. The dinghy pulled up to the cave and Zeb put the motor into neutral. The entrance was sheltered from the worst of the waves here, so Zeb only had to push away from the rock face occasionally.

He worked quickly, setting the central hole of the net in the water and stretching the netting to either side. He tied oversized fishhooks onto the net and jammed them into cracks to secure the whole contraption. Zeb had no idea if strolias would enter the trap opening, if the allure of the cave was enticement enough, but he had no other ideas. Did they only enter the previous cave because he had been chasing

72

them? He wondered what they ate and resolved to put bait in the next cave they came across.

With one last look at his handiwork, Zeb put the motor into drive and roared away. He ground his teeth in frustration. He knew so little. Not for the first time, he cursed his father's tight lips. Zeb was sure his father knew more than he had ever told Zeb. The thought that now his father was dead, and Zeb would never get those answers from him, still hit Zeb like a punch to the gut.

At the boat, Zeb hooked the dinghy back up to the winch and climbed out. Once he had winched the little boat aboard, he poked his head into the lab space.

"Hi, Corrie," he greeted their resident scientist. "You doing okay?" He wanted to hear some encouraging news from somewhere, even if it wasn't about the strolias.

"Yeah, great!" Corrie beamed at him. "Got half of my samples prepped and in the freezer from the last station, and the other half are incubating." She waved at a rack of test tubes under foil on the bench beside her.

"Good, good." Zeb tried to think of a way to segue into his next thought but failed. He spat it out anyway. "So, what do you think the fish we found was? Any educated guesses?"

Corrie's face grew thoughtful and a little guarded, quite unlike her usual open demeanor.

"My best guess is a subspecies of salmon. Maybe a mutation in an isolated population? Salmon always go back to the same river to spawn, so that can create subspecies that don't necessarily interbreed. The morphology is highly unusual, though." She caught Zeb's confusion. "Body form and structure. The coloration, for one. And the horn, of course. I can't fathom the evolutionary pressure that would favor that horn."

"Maybe they use it for fighting, or for defense," Zeb suggested. He didn't mention the poisonous tip.

"Yeah, definitely a possibility." She nodded then

brightened. "I'm running a gel shortly on some DNA I managed to collect from the water in the bucket."

"What does that mean?" Zeb wasn't sure, but he could guess. His heartrate increased.

"If there was enough DNA from the unicorn fish in the water, then we might be able to send it to the university to sequence it, and find out what species it is," she said. "Don't get too excited, it's a ridiculously long shot, but I did get a pellet in my tube after concentrating it, so there is something there. I'm amplifying the DNA with a typical fish sequence, which should show us variations between it and other fish. I'll run the gel soon to see if the DNA is any good."

"Wow," Zeb breathed. He never dreamed that getting genetic information from a bit of seawater was possible. Corrie was looking at his reaction, so he quickly put on an interested but unconcerned expression. She didn't need to know how much this meant to him, not yet. "That's fascinating. Let me know when you find out."

She nodded, and he backed out of the lab space and headed for the wheelhouse. At least he could talk openly with Krista.

KRISTA

Jules poked his head into the wheelhouse where Krista was casually maintaining their position.

"Corrie's in the lab. I'll get lunch going while we're underway."

Krista put the boat into gear and headed to their next destination. She gazed out the window at the ocean beyond. A sailboat inched behind a nearby island, and a ferry chugged away in the distance. Her mind wandered in a half-bored, half-thoughtful state that happened when she drove the boat. It was an unusual frame of mind for her—she was too busy normally to drift like this. It was a waste of time at any other point. But here, that was all there was to do.

She was wondering how her cat was faring, being fed by her neighbor, when Zeb slung himself into the wheelhouse through the outside door and stationed himself at the charts. When it was clear he wasn't going to speak, Krista broke the silence.

"Well? What do you really think the unicorn fish was?"

"It was a strolia," Zeb said. He kept his eyes on the charts. "It had to have been. I've never seen anything like it."

Krista gritted her teeth. Zeb was convinced. That would make her job so much harder. How would she persuade him to give up on this ridiculous mission if it wasn't fruitless after all? She would have to tackle it another day. She changed the topic.

"What do you think of Corrie?"

Zeb took a moment to answer.

"Nice. Normal. Passionate about her work."

Krista made an impatient noise. Typical Zeb, giving such a guarded, bland answer. And nothing about what Krista really cared about.

"Have you asked her yet? About the blog?"

Zeb shook his head.

"I didn't want to scare her off before we'd even left the shore. Let her think that chasing strolias is her idea. I'll stick to my cover story for now."

"You only have a week," Krista said. "If you don't say something, she'll end up leaving the boat without truly helping, and all this effort will be for nothing. Ask her about the blog."

"Today?"

"You might as well. What's she going to do, jump ship? This trip is too important to her work. She'll put up with a lot, I imagine."

They both watched a container ship glide slowly past in the distance.

"I hope you have more of a plan than you've told me," Krista said at last. Zeb was silent, and Krista sighed. "I thought not. How long did you really want to search for? Before I constrained you to the summer?"

"As long as it took." Zeb kept his gaze on the horizon, even though Krista's eyes were burning a hole in his head.

"Or until the money runs out," Krista said. "Which won't be long with gas prices these days."

ZEBALLOS

Krista stopped speaking when Jules' head popped through the doorway.

"Le lunch is served," he said in a terrible French accent.

"Do you remember nothing of your high school French?" Krista asked with a shake of her head. "Astonishing."

"He went to as many French classes as he did of math," Zeb said.

"Zut alors, ze insults I must endure," Jules said with mock-indignation.

"At least you know how to cook," Krista said. "I'll give you that. I'll steer for a while longer, Zeb, if you want to eat. But you'd better save me some."

"Or suffer the wrath of Krista," said Zeb. "Got it."

A smile played on Krista's lips as Zeb and Jules walked through the interior door. Zeb hoped that she would lighten up while they were on the water. She was usually serious, but her severity and nagging were beyond the norm. Zeb knew it was because she was worried for him, but it grated after a while. It took a lot out of him to stay stoic in the face of her dire warnings.

It wasn't as if he hadn't already thought of every objection she came up with, but some things were more important than money. His mother had been different, although she'd tried to hide it. He was different, in ways that only made sense when viewed through the lens of his mother's bedtime stories. Once more, he cursed his father's stubborn secrecy. He had taken knowledge about Zeb to the grave, and now Zeb paid the price. The inheritance money had felt defiled, somehow, as if he were taking a handout from the man he had been at odds with, and who had been as tight-fisted with money as he had been with secrets. Using the money to fund this trip felt right. At least his father would help him find answers in death, if not in life.

"What's for lunch?" Zeb asked to distract himself from his gloomy thoughts.

"Pressed Italian sandwiches," said Jules with a flourish to the galley. "Help yourself. I'm eating on the deck. Coming?"

"I need to talk to Corrie," Zeb said. Jules gave him a look, and Zeb nodded.

"Good luck." Jules took a plate and walked to the door of the makeshift laboratory. "I'll let her know lunch is ready."

Zeb took a plate and squeezed onto the bench surrounding a tiny table. A bundle of charts and old magazines were tucked into a small bungee cord on the side. Zeb pulled out his chart of Vancouver Island and glanced over it while he took a bite of his sandwich.

Corrie entered a few minutes later, looking frazzled but happy.

"Whew! Just processed my samples from the last station. I have some secondary protocols to run, but nothing that can't wait until after lunch. And I started that gel to see if we had enough DNA in the bucket's water to sequence."

"Is it likely?"

"Not really," she said. "But it's worth a try."

"Let's eat while you're waiting. Grab a plate in the galley." Zeb waved his sandwich in the right direction. Corrie retrieved her plate and slid onto the bench across from Zeb.

"This looks amazing." Corrie took a bite.

"Jules' hidden talent. He doesn't have many, but cooking is one. His mum worked away a lot, so he and his dad fended for themselves while he was growing up." Zeb took another bite and swallowed thoughtfully. "He's handy to have on the boat."

"I can see that," said Corrie. "Taste that? Now I'm excited for dinner." She looked at the chart on the table. "What are the stars for?"

Too late, Zeb realized that the chart he was perusing was

liberally marked with pencil indicating places of fascination to his mother—either in story or from brief mentions. They were locations he intended to visit this summer. What he expected to find, even he didn't know. What would he look for? Nevertheless, they were the only clues he had. He stumbled over his words as he waved away her question.

"Oh, well, I don't know. Maybe Dad thought they were good spots to catch halibut. Who knows?" Zeb started to fold the charts. Corrie put out a hand to stop him.

"Can I see? I haven't thought in much detail about sampling locations beyond tomorrow."

Zeb spread the chart out once more and Corrie poured over it, her lunch forgotten. Zeb supposed there was nothing to be gleaned from a few pencil scratches. Besides, he was supposed to talk to Corrie about her fascination with legends. He rolled his shoulders back and attempted to relax his face into a casual expression.

"I'd like to sample Seymour Narrows," Corrie said. Zeb bit back the words he'd been about to say. "Such huge tidal changes there, so dynamic. Pretty interesting, biology-wise, I bet. Do you think it'd be too tricky to sample there?" Corrie's big brown eyes looked hopefully into Zeb's, and he nodded in reassurance.

"We'll manage."

She went back to perusing the chart. There was no time like the present. Zeb cleared his throat.

"Jules found your blog." Zeb winced at his own lack of subtlety. "He's pretty good at finding stuff."

Corrie didn't look up, but her whole face, neck, and even her ears flushed pink. Was she that embarrassed? Zeb felt wrongfooted.

"What do you mean?" Corrie said with an attempt at nonchalance.

"I know you're anonymous on it, but like I said, Jules is good at that. It's really awesome, though, you don't have to hide around here." Zeb floundered. What else could he say? Corrie still wouldn't look at him, and she fidgeted at a tear in the chart with trembling fingers. This was not going as planned. How would he ease her into the idea of helping him if she couldn't even handle a mention of her blog?

She finally looked up at him, and the blood had drained from her face to leave it eerily calm and pale.

"I'm anonymous for a very good reason," she said quietly. "If anyone at the university found out..." She shuddered. "Can you show me how you found out my identity? I obviously need to cover my tracks better."

"Of course," Zeb assured her. "And we won't tell anyone, I promise. I get it—it's not a topic they generally cover in school, is it?" He smiled at her hopefully, and while she didn't return the smile, her features lost their grim fear.

"Why did you pick me for the award, if you knew about the blog?" she said. Her brow creased in a frown. "I don't get it."

"I'm not a scientist. Who's to say you're not onto something? You're definitely thorough." Zeb paused, steeling himself for what he was about to say. "Besides, I found it fascinating. Your description of that mermaid you saw—well, I've heard of others like it. Let's just say I'm a believer."

Corrie's eyes widened, and her fingers gripped the edge of the table.

"Really? Who—what—" She composed herself and spoke more clearly. "I would love to hear any information you have. Stories, legends, friend-of-friend sightings, anything you have. Especially sightings on this coast..." She looked dazzled by the possibilities. "Historical sightings go back millennia in Europe and Asia, but over here, they're so rare. Anything will fatten up my database." She rubbed her face then stared at Zeb through her fingers. "Are you for real? You're not going to go laugh about it with Jules later?"

"No!" Zeb shook his head. "I promise, this is all for real.

80

And if you want to go to any locations for your blog as well as your university project, well…" Zeb spread his hands. "What your professor doesn't know won't hurt him."

Corrie's eyes shone. Her face brightened with a beautiful smile, incredulous yet hopeful all at once. Zeb found himself wanting to make her smile like that again. He hadn't told her his real reason for the award, but it didn't seem necessary. She was as keen as he was to search.

"This will be the best week ever," she said.

CORRIE

Corrie continued to eat her sandwich, but she was quiet and thoughtful now instead of happy. She turned over Zeb's revelation in her mind. When she realized that Zeb was quietly waiting for her to break the silence, she cast about for a new topic.

"Zeballos," she said in a musing tone.

"That's me."

"Why the name? It's unusual, to say the least."

Zeb chuckled.

"Mum and Dad met in Zeballos. It's a tiny place in the middle of nowhere, too small to be called a village, really. Mum had strange ideas about names, and Dad didn't say no." Zeb looked at the sandwich in his hand in contemplation. "At least I can be grateful they didn't meet in Blubber Bay."

Corrie gave an inelegant snort and almost choked on her bite.

"What about Corrie? Is it short for something?" Zeb asked.

Once Corrie had swallowed successfully, she answered with a shrug.

"Short for Coral. It was Dad's idea. Mum named my older sister—Millicent—and Dad wanted a turn."

"You got lucky, I think. Much nicer than Millicent. No offense."

"Yeah, I agree. I don't know what Mum was thinking." Corrie finished the last bite of her sandwich, then her timer started to beep.

"What's that for?" Zeb said.

"Gel's done. I have to see if there's any DNA there from our unicorn fish." Corrie slid out of her seat and rushed to the galley to drop off her dishes in the sink as fast as she could manage with the rocking boat. When she entered the lab space, Zeb was right behind her.

"I'm curious," he said with a sheepish expression when she looked at him. She laughed.

"It will be a while. I'll find you when I'm done, I promise."

Zeb nodded with a disappointed look and walked to the deck. Corrie got to work. She turned off the gel box, then suited up with a lab coat and gloves. The chemicals she used weren't very friendly, and she needed to be careful on the boat. She slipped the gel into a lidded container filled with a staining chemical, then set the timer again and busied herself with her other samples. Her mind was squarely on the gel, though, and when the timer beeped, she dropped her other work and opened the container. Everything was more difficult in her makeshift lab, but she moved the gel into a tiny area on the counter that she had covered with a tent of black plastic. Inside, it was as dark as she could make it. She set up the gel on the ultraviolet light machine, the old spare one her lab used for cruises, and had a look. Her heart sunk.

Instead of a clear band in the gel, which would indicate that her DNA amplification had worked, there was an ugly smear of stained material that lit up under the UV light. She had nothing. Not only did they not have the unicorn fish in a tank, but they didn't even have any genetic material to work with. It had been a faint hope, but a real one. And now, it was crushed.

Corrie threw out the traitorous gel in a hazardous waste container and peeled off her gloves in disgust. She thought she'd be used to the elusiveness of legendary creatures by now, having only ever seen the mermaid in person, but it was almost worse to come so close but not close enough. It was more palatable to deal with second-hand sightings and her data plots than to hold a creature in her hand and then lose it.

She came out onto the deck and saw Zeb leaning over the railing. When he thought no one watched him, he looked as despondent as she felt. Again, she wondered what his background was. There were too many holes in his "rich kid who likes science" story for her to believe.

She leaned against the railing next to him. Before he could ask, she spoke.

"Nothing. I didn't get any DNA."

He sighed and his mouth worked, but he didn't ask about the unicorn fish again.

"Tell me more about your project," he said. Corrie looked at him in surprise. Maybe he did really like science, after all. Zeb gazed at the passing forest on shore, but he seemed attentive. "How is the sampling going so far?"

"Great, really great," she said. "Jules and I have the water sampling figured out. And the next two stations will be very different—one a sheltered bay, one a high-current zone—so that will hopefully give me great contrast with my data. I'm looking forward to collecting some pristine anemone samples instead of the sad specimens near the university."

Behind Zeb, Krista gazed their way with an inscrutable expression. When she caught Corrie looking at her, she nodded and stepped back into the wheelhouse.

"Does your sister not like me?" Corrie asked. She was tired of Krista throwing her dark looks, and she wasn't one to dance around issues. Zeb shifted with discomfort.

"No, it's not that, she's just—don't mind her. It's not you, I promise."

"Good. I'm better at making friends than enemies. Enemies are just friends whom you haven't gone to the right party with yet."

Zeb looked surprised.

"Interesting creed. I can't say I've followed through with

84

that advice before."

"Try it sometime." Corrie grinned. "Everyone has a story, and with a little alcohol and good music, most can be convinced to tell it."

Zeb's smile faded and he looked out to sea once more. Corrie wondered why he was so closed off. It was hard for her to comprehend. She was open with everyone. She didn't understand why someone would limit himself like that.

"What's that?" Zeb gripped the railing and leaned out as far as he could. Corrie followed his eye.

"What?"

"I thought I saw…" Zeb scanned the water, but his shoulders slumped. "I probably imagined it. After seeing the unicorn fish this morning, every flash looks like something strange."

They stood in silence for a moment. Corrie looked down at the wake beside the boat. Her body stiffened and she squeaked out one word.

"Zeb!"

Racing beside the boat were three unicorn fish. They dipped and glided deep below the boat, their horns barely visible in the murky waters and only the occasional flash of rainbow colors winking up at them. Zeb froze, then he jumped back.

"Where's the net?" he yelled. "Quick!"

Corrie raced to the aft deck and fetched the net. Her heart pounded. She pushed the net at Zeb, who lowered it carefully into the water.

"Don't spook them," Corrie whispered. Zeb didn't respond to her obvious comment, and she bit her tongue. He positioned the net near the front of the swimming fish. Corrie figured the rushing water would push the net back and scoop the fish up at the same time.

With a tremendous jab, Zeb plunged the net deep into the water. Corrie couldn't see anything for a few moments except white froth and the net whipping backward. Zeb hauled it out before the water could drag it away.

They stared at the net in disbelief. Its rope netting hung in tatters, and no fish flopped within.

"That damn horn must be sharper than it looks," Zeb said. He brought the net on board and threw it on the ground. His face writhed with emotion before it grew stoic once more. He picked up the net and turned to walk to the aft deck. "Better luck next time. We'll be on station soon. I'll get the dive gear ready."

Corrie blinked at Zeb's contradictory reaction. Sometimes it seemed that he wanted to catch a unicorn fish more than anything, and other times it seemed that he didn't care at all. What was his game?

ZEBALLOS

Jules was sitting on a folding chair on the aft deck when Zeb came around. Zeb brandished the net at him.

"We almost caught one, right now," he said. "The damn thing slashed the net open with its horn."

"What the hell?" Jules reached out to touch the net, but Zeb jerked it out of reach.

"The horns are poisonous," he said. "If my mum was right. Better not touch."

"Go figure." Jules looked at Zeb for a minute. Zeb set the net down and ran his hand through his hair, trying to settle his emotions.

"What?" Zeb said when Jules continued to gaze at him.

"Do you want me to try fishing for one?"

Zeb stared at Jules.

"Yes, brilliant. I have no idea what they like. Try a couple of different lures."

Jules got up slowly and stretched.

"Best case scenario, we catch a unicorn fish. Worst case, we catch dinner."

Zeb climbed into the hold while Jules busied himself with finding fishing rods. They stored the dive gear down there, and a faint aroma of fish lingered that George Artino had never managed to scrub out. It evoked past summers in Zeb and calmed his nerves quickly. The scent, along with Jules' fishing idea, allowed him to compose himself. By the time the boat slowed and Corrie came out of the lab, Zeb had assembled the diving equipment and was relatively tranquil.

"We're on station," Krista's voice crackled through the intercom. "Depth of ten meters. Drop in anytime."

"Suit up," he told Corrie. She grabbed her dry suit from her bag and Zeb stripped down to his swim suit. Jules walked to the aft deck with a fishing rod.

87

"There's speedo boy," Jules said with a laugh. "When are you going to wear shorts like a normal person?"

"Never," Zeb said. "I hate stuffing shorts into a wetsuit." He also hated the extra fabric swirling around his legs when he swam without a wetsuit. It got in the way of all his senses.

"I can't believe you wear a suit that's only three millimeters thick," Corrie said with a shake of her head. "I get cold in my dry suit."

"I don't get cold easily," Zeb said. Truthfully, he didn't need any protection from the cold. He inherited his mother's imperviousness to the cool waters of the local seas, and he only wore the suit to avoid too many awkward questions. But he couldn't bear to wear a suit that was any thicker than what he already owned—it was enough that he couldn't feel the play of water on his skin, let alone feel the restriction of a thicker neoprene. He didn't want her to dwell on his comment, so he quickly deflected. "What's the plan?"

Corrie started to check the equipment on his back while she spoke.

"Dive down to the ocean floor, head east along the edge of the shelf until we see some plumose anemones. I'll take some samples, and then we'll head back." She pressed a button on Zeb's equipment and air hissed out. "You're all set."

Zeb checked over Corrie's equipment, then they waddled backward to the edge of the boat in their flippers. Jules clipped his fishing rod to the railing and opened a door in the side of the boat for an easier drop. Zeb went first, his skin itching to submerse itself in the water.

He fell, and with a jolting splash a world of cool green enveloped him. His heartrate immediately dropped, and tension released from his shoulders that he hadn't realized he'd been carrying. His head popped out of the surface, and he winced at the noise and light. Corrie was waiting, so he swam to the side, the tank on his back dragging him uncomfortably.

"Geronimo!" Corrie said, her voice muffled from the snorkel in her mouth. She fell backward with a huge splash, then bobbed up right away. Her eyes were merry behind her mask. "Ready, captain?"

Zeb gave the hand signal for down and let air hiss out of his jacket. It felt more natural to use hand signals underwater. Sometimes, he preferred it. Everyone loved to talk, talk, talk, all the time. Even Jules, while often content to let a comfortable silence reign, talked more than Zeb wanted sometimes. He missed that about his mother. They would go for days without saying anything aloud to each other. They spoke plenty, with little hand signs that she had made up, or with subtle cues in body language that his father had never understood, but spoken word was not their primary mode of communication. Zeb preferred it.

They descended into the dim, green water. He hated diving with a wetsuit and a tank. It was so cumbersome, restrictive, and noisy. He didn't need any of it. True, he could only hold his breath for ten minutes, not the forty minutes that he could last with a tank of air, but there was nothing stopping him from diving multiple times. Not only that, but he couldn't feel anything with the suit on. He was effectively blind to the delicate currents of water that told him so much when he free dived.

No matter. This was a job, like any other. He had led plenty of dive groups previously, under his father's direction. When George had phased out of fishing, he had filled some of the void with charter trips. While the diving gear was uncomfortable, it was familiar.

Zeb followed Corrie's lead. He was only there for emergency support, because no one should dive alone. Corrie had her mission, and he bobbed along in her wake like a towed dinghy. A school of perch floated beside him, and he snapped his head around. What if strolias were swimming here? He scanned the murky water, but no rainbow glimmer met his searching eyes. Maybe the fish were scared off by their bubbles.

There was a clump of anemones up the slope to their left, and Corrie swam slowly in that direction. She pulled out large-handled clippers from a mesh sack attached to her vest and cut a small frond off the nearest anemone. The anemone shrank into itself, but Corrie ushered the tiny white piece of material into a plastic bag before tucking it into her sack. She repeated this twice more, then indicated to Zeb to follow her.

They collected from three clusters before Corrie was finished. Zeb led the way back to the boat, his sense of direction hampered by his gear but still more acute than Corrie's. When they surfaced, Corrie was beaming.

"That was an amazing haul! This is incredible. I could hug you, Zeb. This is the best week ever."

Her grin was infectious. Despite Zeb's worries, anger, and disappointment, his face cracked into a smile at her happiness.

"Glad I could help," he said.

"I'd better take my water samples now. Wow, I hope I don't mess that up. The dive was so good!"

Jules appeared at the top of the ladder he had attached to the side for them, and Corrie continued to babble about their dive to his appreciative ear as she ascended. Zeb felt the pull of the ocean when he climbed the ladder, like the hands of a departing lover. He felt it every time he came back to the surface, and his skin crawled with the need to feel the cool salt water on his skin, unhindered by neoprene.

He stripped off the offending material on the aft deck and shoved the gear out of the way. He would clean it later. He wrapped a towel around his middle and walked to the bow, leaving Jules and Corrie to put the collection bottle in the water with the winch. He slid a hand behind the life ring to extract a pair of streamlined flippers, the small ones that competitive swimmers sometimes used. On the bow, he ditched his towel, slipped on the flippers, and climbed the railing.

"Really?"

Zeb swung his head around. Krista leaned against the outside of the wheelhouse with her arms crossed and a disbelieving look on her face.

"What?" he said. "Corrie's busy. And I want to see if I can find a strolia. They're everywhere these days, apparently."

Krista was not deceived.

"You really can't hold out for one week?"

Zeb rubbed his arm unconsciously.

"I'll only be a few minutes." He didn't wait to hear a response. Instead, he straightened, took a deep breath, then dived into the waves with hardly a splash.

The relief flooded his body, and his heartrate dropped once more. Cool water caressed his bare skin with a thousand tiny touches, each current a slightly different temperature and salinity. Instantly, he could sense the lay of the land, where the currents rushed by in the strait, where there were pockets of stagnant cave water, where rock formations interrupted smooth wave action. A ling cod moved in a lazy spiral nearby, and Zeb felt it without looking.

It wasn't quiet down here, although it was a different quality of sound. There was a distant roaring gurgle of waves on the shore and moans and clicks of creatures both swimming and attached to rocks. Far in the distance, a porpoise pod whistled among themselves. These sounds were what Zeb heard in his dreams.

Once his body had equilibrated and he felt centered and peaceful, he kicked himself forward. Water rushed past his skin, telling him new information with every thrust forward. He closed his eyes and scanned for fish-like disturbances.

Three rockfish to his left, perch above, and octopus in a cave nearby, but nothing unusual, nothing that would indicate strolias. An empty moon snail shell gleamed on the sand below him, and he kicked down to pick it up. He already had a few moon snails, but this might be his largest yet. It would look good on his shelf at home. Mindful of Corrie's sampling time and his promise to Krista, Zeb swam for only a few minutes before turning back in resignation.

The boat was a dark oval above him, its shadow looming large on the seafloor. Zeb swam up to the bow then stopped. There was something attached to the hull. He swam closer.

It was small, about the size of his outstretched hand, with a streamlined cover to reduce drag. Zeb ran his fingers on the smooth surface and tried to find a handle or way to open the cover, but there was nothing.

The cover pulsed. A shudder ran through Zeb's body, and at the faintest edge of his hearing there was a low moan. He stared at the device in astonishment. Had the noise come from it?

Zeb waited for another minute. The device pulsed every ten seconds, but nothing responded to the noise. Was it some sort of sonar that his father had installed? He wondered where in the wheelhouse the instrumentation was for this device, then he scowled. His father was too secretive for his own good.

Zeb surfaced with a huge gulp of fresh air. Krista peered over the railing.

"Over this side," she said with a wave. "They're still sampling."

Zeb struck out for the starboard side, where Krista had left the ladder installed for him. He crept swiftly up the ladder, the pull of the ocean a familiar ache as his body slid out of the water. Corrie had her back to the bow while she fiddled with the collection bottle. Jules grinned at him then gave a thumbs up. Zeb rolled his eyes at his friend and went to find his discarded towel.

MATHIAS

Matt looked around. His nose didn't wrinkle in disgust, but it was a close thing. A short chain-link fence surrounded the front yard of a tiny bungalow. It enclosed ratty grass, bare mud patches, and piles of junk. He counted three open refrigerators, five bicycles, and an old Ford pickup on blocks. The only life thriving in the yard was a multitude of yellow dandelions.

The house was in a similar state of mismanagement. Bedraggled curtains hung behind grimy windowpanes, and one window was boarded up altogether. Paint peeled off the wooden slats of the siding. Matt compared the bungalow to his snug little house that he had bought last year. While a similar size to this one, Matt cared for his first home carefully. Bianca liked it too—she said it was a perfect little starter house—although she clearly expected to get a bigger one when they moved on with their relationship. Matt hadn't planned on it, but he supposed she might have a point. Too bad, though, he really loved the little house, with its white trim and snug woodstove.

When Matt stepped up three steps to the porch, a disconcerting groan made him freeze. When he didn't fall through, he gingerly walked to the front door. He ignored the doorbell—the chances were low of it actually working—and rapped sharply on the door.

It took a full minute and two more knocks before the door squealed open. Matt waited patiently and did his best to look unthreatening, a difficult proposition with his chiseled Nordic features and well-muscled shoulders. He hoped this was the right house. He wanted to get this over with and get back home to Bianca.

This is for Bianca, he reminded himself. *When the money starts rolling in, she'll be happy as a clam. Man up, Matt, and do the deal.*

A short, wiry man peered out at Matt with bleary eyes. He was in his thirties, with a few days' worth of stubble on his chin and a potent scent of alcohol that Matt could smell from his vantage point. His nose threatened to wrinkle again. He quashed the urge.

"Kiefer Nolan?" Matt said pleasantly.

The man looked him up and down, and a tinge of wariness entered his bloodshot eyes.

"Yeah? What?" Kiefer said in a high-pitched voice. Matt took a deep breath and then wished he hadn't.

"I was told you were the man to talk to, if I have product I want to push. I know you know people, know where to go."

"Who sent you?" Kiefer demanded. He planted his feet squarely, whether to fight or run, Matt wasn't sure.

"Tom Banks told me," Matt said quickly. Kiefer relaxed and let the door swing open more. A musty smell wafted from the dim hallway beyond.

"You should have started with that. Come in, come in."

Matt stepped over the threshold after a moment's hesitation. *For Bianca*, he reminded himself firmly. That engagement ring she'd been hinting about wasn't going to buy itself. Matt was lucky to have his beautiful girlfriend, and a pretty ring to commemorate their commitment to each other shouldn't be too big of an ask. Even if the requested rock was the size of the Hope diamond.

Kiefer led the way to a small kitchen in the back. Matt didn't bother to remove his shoes. Dishes were piled in the sink and the table was covered in a miasma of plates and old newspapers, but Kiefer pushed the detritus to one side and motioned Matt to sit.

"So, what do you got?" Kiefer said when they were seated. "Don't say you've started growing weed in your basement. I used to get that all the time. Stuff was always crap. That shit's legal now, though."

"No, not marijuana. This is entirely new." Matt pulled out a plastic self-sealing baggie with a tiny amount of white powder in it. "It's derived from an ocean product, but I don't want to say more."

"Yeah, yeah, trade secrets. I got it." Kiefer took the bag from Matt and held it up to examine it. "What does it do?"

"Hallucinations. Really wild visions. No side effects in any of the test subjects so far." Only he, his cousin Pete, and Larry and his friends had tested it, and everyone seemed fine. That was test enough for Matt.

"Nice. Do you have a name for it?"

"Uh…" Should Matt have a name handy? He hadn't thought that far ahead. This was the first product he had developed, after all. He suppressed the urge to laugh wildly.

"How about Sea Salt?" Kiefer said. "Makes sense for looks and origin. Plus, it's catchy. Is this a dose? Do you eat it or snort it?"

"Eat it, and that dose will last for about half an hour."

"I'll have to put it on something edible," Kiefer mused. "No one will know what to do with a powder. What do you want to sell it for?"

Matt shrugged helplessly. He really was out of his depth here. Kiefer leaned forward.

"Look, here's what we'll do," he said, all business. "Sell it cheap at first, get the word out. Not too cheap, you still want to make a profit, but as low as you can manage. Then we jack up the price. You got lots?"

"I can get it," said Matt. The weird fish with the horns always came for his bait. They hadn't failed him yet.

"Awesome. Leave me with a couple of testers and I'll buy five doses for sale. If I like it, I'll start selling it. Give me your number and I'll call you when I need more."

Matt walked out of the ramshackle bungalow a few baggies lighter and with an uncertain hope in his chest. His plan might just work. It was too late to back out now, anyway. It had been too late when he had bought all that equipment for Pete, his pharmacist cousin, to prepare the product. It was money or bust, now.

CORRIE

Corrie finally finished her last sample prep in the lab and let out a huge sigh. Dinner had been a hurried affair during a quick incubation break. She hoped Jules hadn't been too offended when she scarfed down the herb-crusted halibut. She had tried to tell him how delicious it was, but she wasn't sure that he had understood her through her mouthful as she bolted back to the lab to the incessant beeping of her timer. Luckily, she got the impression that he didn't offend easily.

She stripped off her gloves with relief and rubbed her clammy hands together. She was toast. Time to check her email and head to bed. Jules and Zeb were playing cards in the galley and Krista was reading in their shared cabin, so Corrie pulled out her laptop from a drawer and connected it to her phone to access the internet.

First, she wanted to write a quick blog post. There was so much to say, but she kept it brief.

Everyone, I might be onto something big. I'm on the ocean right now, and we've sighted a creature that is not known to exist. It looks like a rainbow-colored salmon with a horn, and we saw a whole school of them. We're calling them unicorn fish, for lack of a better term. They're unreal. I'll update you when I find out more. Has anyone heard of a legend like this? Reply in the comments!

There were a few emails from the university, nothing earth-shattering, and an email from Adrianna. Corrie smiled and opened it.

Hi Corrie, we miss you already! Check out Koni's picture he drew for you. It's on our living room wall now. Pizza night when you get back? Adrianna

The picture was a black and white cartoon of a plumose anemone sporting a goofy grin and a pair of sunglasses. Corrie snorted out loud. Her roommates were ridiculous, and she loved them.

YES! to pizza. And I love the picture. That one looks much happier than the ones I'm snipping bits off, though. Corrie

The last message was from her supervisor. Corrie's stomach dropped. Jonathan didn't email her often, but she never liked it when he checked up on her. She always felt that she should have been doing more between meetings, collecting more data, producing more figures. This email was no different.

Corrie, Congrats on your first day at sea. Send me a progress update as soon as you can. Jonathan

Corrie sighed and pulled up some numbers from her first bits of data that she had measured today. There wasn't much—most of her work would be done in the lab when she got home—but she had some information. She cobbled together a quick bar graph of temperatures and salinity profiles, dashed off some notes about diving conditions, and pressed send.

Not two minutes later, she received a reply.

That's a good start. I'd like to see some preliminary data from your anemone collections, to see if we're on the right path. Run a gel to make sure you're getting the DNA you expect. If it's not there, we might have to re-think your collection methods on the fly. Jonathan

Corrie's heart sank. That sort of analysis wasn't trivial, and there were only so many hours in the day. Sampling took up most of her time.

Then she remembered that she had found time to run a gel today, to check for genetic material in the unicorn fish's seawater. She slumped in defeat. Was her hunt for the unicorn fish already getting in the way of her real science collection?

Finding the unicorn fish was the chance of a lifetime and had huge potential repercussions for both her and the world. But, this week of cruising was also an incredible opportunity for her science career, one she didn't want to squander. Her work on the anemones was important and had a more likely payoff for her career and for society. She couldn't afford to waste this time.

She would simply have to do both. She could work longer and harder. It was only a week, after all. She could sleep when she got home.

Reluctantly, but with more resolve, she took some samples out of her tiny bar fridge and got to work.

ZEBALLOS

Zeb lay awake on his bunk long after Jules' breathing grew even and deep. The waters of the calm bay they were anchored in hadn't soothed him with their gentle rocking. He flipped over in his bunk with a frustrated sigh. Searching for strolias had awakened in him so many buried memories. His mother, with her gray eyes so like his, in a pale face so unlike, had understood him in ways no one else seemed to. If she had still been alive, Zeb could have simply asked her for the truth. Instead, he was relegated to scratching for clues in silt while blindfolded. Anger bubbled up inside him at his father for hoarding secrets like a miser.

Then, the anger melted away when he realized that they were both gone now. There was no one to look up to, and no one to blame. There was only him and the two-dimensional memories of his parents in his mind. Despite Jules' soft breathing above him, he felt more profoundly alone than he'd ever had.

Zeb cursed softly under his breath and rolled out of bed. There was no point lying here, sleepless and with no hope of reaching that state. He pulled open a drawer, took out his whistle, and gently slid the drawer closed. He crept outside in loose shorts, with no shirt and bare feet.

Moonlight caught the whistle in its beam, and the instrument gleamed a luminescent white. It was made from the rib bone of a *callo*, his mother had told him, accompanied by her chortling laugh. It was the length of Zeb's forearm, thin and curved, with carved swirls and lines on the surface. Zeb ran his fingers over the markings with familiarity. His mother had taught him to play the whistle when he was three, and its haunting notes had often been the last sound he'd heard at night. His father had refused to hear it after she had died, so Zeb had made a habit of swimming out to an isolated

100

outcrop on Quadra Island to play when he needed to hear his mother's voice.

Zeb walked to the bow and sat on the windlass. He brought the whistle to his lips and began to play.

Echoing notes bounced off the nearby forest and drifted over shallow waves. The sound the whistle made was breathy and soft, more haunting than piercing. Almost, if someone were listening from afar, they might mistake it for a keening wind or the far-off cry of a gray whale. Like his mother had taught him, Zeb didn't play any recognizable tune. Notes floated past each other, up and down, long and short, with no discernable rhythm, yet the whole evoked a sense of melancholy that suited Zeb's mood perfectly.

He played for longer than he had planned to. The music calmed him and allowed his mind to drift peacefully instead of thrashing around in the storm. When he finally put the whistle down, lapping waves played a different music. Zeb closed his eyes, trying and failing to ignore the call of the sea. When he couldn't resist any longer—didn't want to resist— he stripped off his shorts and dived overboard.

The water washed away the last lingering tension that his music hadn't removed. Currents swept over him, around him, and he finally relaxed. His fingers dragged through the water and a million points of light sparkled like fairy dust over his skin from phosphorescent plankton. His mouth widened in a true smile, one that he rarely showed above the waves. Then he spun around in the water for the sheer joy of it, watching the bioluminescence swirl in his wake.

JULES

Jules woke to the familiar sound of Zeb's whistle. If he hadn't known what it was, he might have slept through it or thought it was the wind, although the night was still. The unearthly music flowed into the cabin, faint and ghostly.

Zeb had been more serious than usual the past few months, ever since he had blown up at his father about keeping secrets. If Zeb had been a loose cannon, Jules might have worried that he would have punched a wall. As it was, Zeb had swum away for three days, long enough for even the laid-back Jules to think about calling the coast guard. When Zeb finally emerged, dripping wet at Jules' trailer door, Jules had let him in, and he'd slept for twenty-four hours straight.

Zeb, in his typical fashion, had only outlined the bare bones of his fight with his father, but Jules was adept enough at reading between Zeb's lines to hear the whole story. George Artino wasn't an easy man to live with and was closed-mouthed at the best of times, let alone about the kind of things Zeb wanted him to talk about.

Now, months later, the strain of finding answers was still eating Zeb up. Jules didn't know how to help, beside coming on this trip.

The music would help. It always did. Jules turned on his side and waited for it to stop, for Zeb to come back to bed.

Twenty minutes later, the echoing notes faded. When no Zeb darkened the doorway, Jules climbed off the top bunk and threw on a thick sweater. The spring night air was cold on the water, despite warm days. Not all of them were lucky enough to be impervious to the cold. If Jules were a jealous man, he would have said goodbye to Zeb long ago.

The bow was empty, but Jules found a comfortable spot leaning against the wheelhouse and waited. Sure enough, after a half hour, the clink of metal ladder on hull sounded from the starboard side, and Zeb wandered to the bow to find his discarded shorts. He jumped when Jules gave a quiet wolf-whistle.

"Hiya, handsome," he said in a falsetto voice. In his normal pitch he said, "But please, pants on."

"I was alone," Zeb grumbled. He wriggled his shorts over wet legs then sat down next to Jules. "What are you doing up?"

"Someone was moaning like a beached whale out here. I came to investigate."

Zeb huffed.

"Luckily, I play for myself, not for my adoring audience."

"Don't quit your day job," Jules said. He glanced sideways at Zeb. "You figure anything out?"

Zeb shrugged. He looked calmer than this afternoon. He always seemed to after swimming. Jules wondered what he did down there. He had no interest in joining Zeb on his little expeditions—it was cold enough on land without jumping in an ice bath like the ocean in spring—but he was curious all the same. Not curious enough to find out, though. Jules had limits, and comfort usually took priority over curiosity.

"We'll keep at it," Jules said, leaving Zeb to figure out whether he meant finding the strolias, helping Corrie, or life in general. He wasn't sure himself. "But stressing over something you can't control doesn't help."

"Easier said than done."

"Yeah, true." Jules was struck by a brilliant idea. "You know what, we all need to unwind. You're stressed about the strolias, Corrie's stressed about her science stuff, and Krista always has something stuck up her ass. After our last station tomorrow, we'll be really close to Lasqueti Island. I say we go to the pub there tomorrow night."

Zeb looked unimpressed.

"I guess we could."

"Yeah, it'll be great! It's just what you need. First drinks are on me." Zeb looked at him with incredulity. Jules amended his statement. "After you give me an advance on my pay, of course."

Finally, a grin cracked Zeb's face.

"Yeah, you're on."

CORRIE

Corrie was dragged out of a dead sleep by the sound of Krista banging drawers closed in their shared cabin.

"Izzit morning already?" she croaked. She hadn't made it to bed until late, then she had woken at three in the morning to check on a sample run. Hopefully she would survive this week. If every day was like yesterday, it would be a very long week indeed. She wondered if Jules had packed enough coffee in the galley.

Krista pulled on a sweater and ran a wet comb over her short hair.

"We're pulling up anchor in a minute, and we'll be at the station in half an hour. So, get dressed, get breakfast, and be ready to dive. Chop chop."

With those soft words of encouragement, Krista left the cabin. Corrie groaned and rubbed her aching eyes. She could do this. She was strong. She was tough. Nothing could get in between her and her science.

No one was in the galley when she emerged from her cabin, although shouts and clanking from the deck told her where the rest of the crew was. She moaned in ecstasy at the sight of a large pot of hot coffee.

"I think I might be falling in love with Jules," she murmured. "Or at least his cooking."

She shoved a plateful of prepared toast and eggs in her mouth, appreciating the delicate fluffiness of the eggs as she did so. Finally, fortified with breakfast and two cups of strong coffee, she walked outside to the aft deck.

The boat was already underway, and trees slid by on the shore as they passed. Jules was in the hold, lifting out diving gear.

"Your talents are wasted here," Corrie called down. "Those eggs were amazing."

105

Jules looked up with a grin.

"Good eggs are too easy to make. It's criminal to rubberize an egg. Think of all the work the poor chicken had to do for it."

"True." Corrie yawned then squatted down to attach her diving vest to one of the tanks. "When did you get up to make breakfast? I probably would have slept forever if Krista hadn't woken me."

Jules shrugged and hauled a weight belt out of the hold.

"Dunno. Early. That's the schedule on the boat. Zeb's dad always ran it like that, and I guess the apple doesn't fall far from the tree." He looked past Corrie with a mischievous twinkle in his eye as he spoke, and Corrie looked around. Zeb stood there with a disgruntled look on his face. He huffed.

"That's a low blow, Jules." He looked at Corrie. His eyes were tired and a little sad around the edges, but he seemed calmer than yesterday, less on edge. "We're up early because you have a lot of places you want to go, and it takes time to travel between them. And we only have a week, right? Make hay while the sun shines."

"Yes," Corrie said with resolution. "That's exactly right. This is my trip of a lifetime, and I can't waste it by sleeping. Just keep making that strong coffee, Jules, and I will survive."

The station ran smoothly, much like the day before. Corrie and Zeb dived to collect anemone fronds, then Jules helped Corrie send down her bottles to collect water. When the last bottle was on deck, a splash made Corrie's head whip around.

"What was that? Did something fall overboard?" Corrie counted her bottles to make sure.

"Probably just a fish jumping," Jules said. "They're frisky in the morning. Should we take these bottles into the lab?"

"Yes, please. Then I might find Zeb and talk about the next station."

"You know what, I'll find him and send him to the lab,

106

okay?" Jules said quickly. Corrie shrugged.

"Sure, that works. I'll start filtering my water."

Jules retreated to the wheelhouse and Corrie was left to wonder at Jules' reaction. What was Zeb doing that Jules didn't want her to know about?

She shook her head. Likely he was down tinkering with the engine or something noisy and smelly that she didn't need to bug him at. She pulled on gloves and got to work.

The rest of the day was a blur of diving, sampling, analysis, and running gels. At one point, they passed one of the caves in which Zeb had fashioned a net trap for the unicorn fish. When he returned from checking it, his face was even more closed than usual, and Corrie didn't enquire about his success. It was too evident from his despondent expression. She hardly had time to ask, in any event. They tackled three stations in total, and by dinnertime Corrie was exhausted and ready to drop. She needed to get out of the lab, talk to a human about anything. Science was often solitary, and while she worked well in her own thoughts, she needed to recharge with company.

As if she'd spoken the thought aloud, Jules appeared and leaned against the doorframe of the lab. He looked at her equipment with interest.

"Anything I can help you with?"

Corrie looked up from her pipetting. Her mouth formed an automatic "no," but she paused. Was there something non-technical that he could do? She wanted to finish up as quickly as possible, and everything took so much time.

"If you have steady hands and can squeeze into gloves, you can put these tubes in a rack. That would be amazing."

Jules sauntered over to the glove box and struggled to fit his hand into her medium-sized latex gloves. Gloves finally on, he stood expectantly before her.

"Once the rack is full, take this water and pour ten milliliters into each tube."

Jules was careful and dexterous, a surprise to Corrie until she remembered his skill in the kitchen. His easy-going slacker demeanor hadn't led her to expect it. She continued her work, but it was a relief to chat to someone while she did so. She had been too long on her own today.

They were finishing up their respective tasks when Krista stopped by the lab.

"She's got you working already, Jules," she said. "Is it a new calling for you? Maybe you shouldn't have skipped your science classes in high school, too. You might have liked them."

"Some of my high school science was interesting," Corrie said, wanting to come to Jules' defense, although he didn't seem perturbed. "But I really got my love of science from my dad. He's a chemist and was forever experimenting in his shed in the yard. Lots of explosions and funny smells."

"See, if class had been like that, I might have stuck around," Jules said with a laugh. "But we can't all be mad scientists, or high-power lawyer types like you, Krista. Someone needs to do odd jobs. Might as well be me."

"Minimum effort, maximum free time," Krista said, but without real rancor. It sounded to Corrie as if this was a conversation that the two had argued many times in the past.

"Zeb and I are thinking of going to the Lasqueti pub tonight," Jules announced. "Who's in?"

"A pub? Here?" Corrie was flabbergasted. "Where is it?"

"On Lasqueti Island. There are a few local islanders who go, but mostly the customers are boaters. It's pretty lively, decent food. At least until they shut off the power at night."

"Yes," Corrie breathed. That was exactly what she wanted tonight. Leave the boat, blow off some steam, see other people. "I am in."

Krista looked disgruntled.

"I don't know. I'm not really interested."

"I didn't make dinner," said Jules. "So, it'll have to be

cold cuts if you want to eat."

Krista gave a long-suffering sigh.

"Fine," she said. "But I'm only coming for the food."

Krista left, and a few minutes later, Jules stood up.

"Is that all of them?" He waved at the tubes in front of him. They were neatly arranged and filled. Corrie sighed with relief at a task she didn't have to do.

"Yes, you're a lifesaver, Jules. I'm almost done here. Thanks for helping."

"Anytime. I'll be prepping breakfast in the galley if you need more help."

Jules stripped off his gloves and disappeared through the doorway. Corrie pipetted a few more samples, then her cell phone rang. She stared at it in surprise. She wasn't expecting anyone to call her on the boat. She carefully placed her samples in a rack and took off one glove to answer the phone. It was David.

"Hi, David."

"Hi babe," he replied. Corrie blinked at the new nickname, but let it slide without comment. He must be missing her. "I thought I'd try you. You've had your phone off since you got on the boat."

"No, but cell range is intermittent out here." How many times had he tried to call? "I'm sure I mentioned that. How are you?"

"Good, good. Just wanted to hear your voice. How is the sampling?"

"So great." She had no intention of telling him about the unicorn fish. He wouldn't believe her. Who would? When she had firmer evidence, maybe she would tell him. Until then, it was a fairy tale. "Lots of great samples, and the diving is spectacular. We had three stations today, and I'm totally wiped. We're going to a pub tonight—only accessible by boat, can you imagine—so I'm looking forward to letting off some steam there. I would kill for a beer right now."

"You're going out drinking, you and the captain?" David said.

"Yeah, and the crew." Corrie narrowed her eyes, but said only, "Should be good. Anyway, I need to finish up my samples, but I'll email you soon, okay?"

When they had said their goodbyes and she had hung up, Corrie stared at her phone for a minute. Did she really seem that loose, that David should be so worried about her going to a pub with the crew? Jealousy was an ugly color on David, and she resolved to ignore the last bit of their conversation. She'd give him the benefit of the doubt.

ZEBALLOS

Krista walked into the wheelhouse. She wore jeans and a T-shirt, as she always did on the boat, except that the jeans were fitted dark denim and the shirt was tighter than what she usually wore. She had even done something to her eyes with makeup.

"Big night on the town?" Zeb said. Krista scowled.

"You might be okay with salty hair and grunge, but I like to clean up sometimes."

"It's nothing to do with the owner of the pub?" Zeb knew Krista used to have a crush on Phillip in high school. Phillip had bought the pub a few years ago. Krista, being Krista, had been far too abrasive to consider ever telling him her feelings. Zeb was certain that Phillip would never have guessed in his wildest dreams. It might have been over ten years ago, but old habits die hard.

"I have no interest in Phillip," she said stiffly. "That doesn't mean I want to look like a slob in front of him. I have an image to uphold. You might consider cleaning up yourself." She looked pointedly at his torn jeans and plaid shirt. Zeb looked down at his clothes and shrugged.

"It's just Lasqueti."

"Go on." Krista grabbed the wheel and waved him out the door. "Honestly. No wonder you don't have a girlfriend."

"Hey, that's not fair," Zeb protested. "There are other reasons for that."

"Yeah, yeah. But the clothes don't help."

Zeb glared at Krista, but she ignored him to stare out the windshield. Zeb clattered back into the cabin area with practiced ease, still annoyed by Krista's comment. It wasn't that he hadn't been approached by any women. His strange looks were off-putting to some and attractive to others, and he'd had a few flings chartering the boat with female divers

111

who were entranced by his ease and grace in the water. There had even been a steady girlfriend just out of high school. The relationship had lasted until she went away to university and left him in their small town working for his father.

The problem was, he was different. Krista's fear for him, of others finding out his strangeness and exploiting it, had infected him over the years until he never considered even trying a relationship with someone. Besides, he was fine on his own. Someone else would get in his way, crowd his thoughts, talk too much, ask too many questions. He didn't need that. He liked the freedom to swim away whenever he wanted.

Zeb rifled through his drawers until he found his least ripped jeans and a shirt that wasn't plaid. It would have to do. He threw the clothes on, took a cursory glance in the mirror to make sure his short hair was in place, and went to find the others.

Jules was perched on a stool in the lab while Corrie put racks of tubes in the fridge. They were chatting up a storm, and Zeb's skin itched. So much sound—he wanted to be in the water again.

"We're almost there," he said when there was a break in the conversation. "Nearly ready?"

"Yes," said Corrie. She removed her gloves with a snap and threw them in a garbage pail with a satisfied look on her face. "Done and done. For the next three hours, anyway. I'm starving. Let me go change and I'll be up in five minutes."

She rushed out of the lab. Jules swiveled on the stool.

"She knows what she's doing," he said in a musing tone. "All sorts of different tests and samples she's collecting. She has a plan, a bigger picture, you know? She's going places."

"She's on a mission," Zeb agreed, not sure where Jules was going with this.

"Yes, exactly." Jules looked thoughtful, then he laughed. "Way too much like work. Type A, am I right? Come on, let's get the dinghy winched out."

They anchored in a wide bay. At the head, a long dock jutted out from shore, where a large building shone with welcoming lights, and faint strains of music drifted over the lapping waves. Zeb could almost smell the food from here, and his stomach rumbled.

Corrie strode onto the deck in a tight black skirt and form-fitting red V-neck. Corrie caught Zeb looking and looked defiant.

"My roommate made me pack it. All my other clothes are too utilitarian for dinner out."

"It's not that kind of place," Zeb said. Privately, he thought the skirt suited her well. Jules, of course, had more appropriate words.

"I think you look far too classy for this old dump." Jules waved at the pub, then held his hand out for Corrie to grab. "But they will feed us, so we might as well grace them with our presence."

Corrie giggled and hopped into the dinghy. The rest piled in. Zeb squeezed next to Jules on the stern to pull the motor's cord, and they roared away to the allure of food.

The pub was busy, with customers spilling out onto picnic tables in front to enjoy the warm spring weather. Krista took the lead and marched across the porch to the front door. Her head was high and her shoulders back, and Zeb knew that she was scanning the room for Phillip so she would know exactly where to aim her most aloof look.

Jules greeted the bartender like an old friend, although Zeb was sure they had never met.

"What's your poison, Corrie?" Jules asked in a hearty voice. An almost unnoticeable wince crossed Corrie's face, before she answered in a hearty tone to match Jules' own.

"Any pale ale." She turned to Zeb. "Zeb?"

"Two lagers." He indicated to Krista and himself, and the bartender nodded. Krista's eyes were still scanning the room and she hadn't noticed their exchange, but Zeb knew what his sister drank.

"Hey!" Jules grabbed his drink and moved toward a table in the corner. Three men yelled their greetings at him. "Long time, no see!"

"Find a table?" Zeb asked Corrie. She sipped her drink and nodded.

"Yeah, definitely. My feet are killing me."

"I'm going for a walk," Krista announced. "If you order something, get me a burger. I'll see you in a bit." She grabbed her beer and headed outside. Corrie looked confused.

"Wow. I know she doesn't like me, but that was obvious, even for her."

"What?" Zeb looked in surprise at Corrie, then frowned after his sister. "No, she doesn't not like you, it's just—complicated," he ended lamely. Corrie raised her eyebrows.

"Whatever. It's no skin off my back. Come on, let's find a table. Look! I think they're leaving."

Corrie bounced over to the emptying table and deftly slid into a chair with a sweet smile at the departing group. Zeb joined her and wondered what to say. He wasn't that great at small talk to begin with, and the only topics they had in common were science, of which they were ridiculously mismatched, and strolias, which they probably shouldn't discuss in public. Luckily, Corrie had no conversational inhibitions.

"This place is great! I love how it's only accessible by boat. I remember, this one time…" She filled Zeb's silence, and Zeb was relieved that his contributions were limited to appearing interested and occasionally agreeing. It was by turns fascinating and comforting to let Corrie speak uninterrupted. Would she end naturally at some point, or did she have an infinite number of things to say? She tucked a piece of her brown hair behind her ear, and he wondered idly if it was as silky as it looked.

"What's your stake in our little fish problem?" Corrie asked. "You're pretty invested. I know my reasons, but what are yours?"

Zeb floundered. Why didn't he have an answer at hand? Of course, she would be interested in that. It was a wonder that this was the first time she had asked.

Jules chose that moment to reappear, and Zeb sighed in relief. Corrie gave him a sharp look but let the subject slide. Bobbing in Jules' wake was a middle-aged man, pot-bellied and gray-haired. He beamed affably with the expression of someone already well-acquainted with the bar. Jules held two more drinks in his hands.

"Don't forget to pay the tab, captain," Jules said with a grin at Zeb, who shot his friend a look of resignation. Jules was always friendlier than he had cash to support. Zeb didn't mind much. Without Jules, he wouldn't have many friends. His exuberant partner-in-crime brought him out into the world, and a few beers was a small price to pay. He didn't have to pretend to like it, though.

"And who's your friend?" Corrie asked.

"This is Larry," Jules said with a gesture not unlike a farmer showing off a prize cow. He sat in one of the empty chairs and set a beer in front of another one. Larry sat with a bemused air but wrapped his hand around the beer with a speed Zeb hadn't expected from an inebriated middle-aged man. "I was talking to Darryl and Lily, over there." Jules waved vaguely backward. "And they told me about a fisherman who caught something really weird the other day."

Jules paused to give Zeb a significant look. Zeb leaned forward despite himself. He had assumed Larry was one of Jules' "great new friends" that he always picked up for a conversation or two on nights out. Zeb hadn't expected to hear anything interesting.

"Then, lo and behold," Jules continued, slapping Larry on the back and making his beer slop over the table. "There he

115

was, the man of the hour himself!"

"Wow, what did you catch?" Corrie said with a flirtatious lean-in. "I love a good sailor's yarn. Can you spin me a tale, Larry?"

Zeb was impressed. Corrie looked like a flirting young woman, and Larry was lapping it up. Only Zeb could see the intensity behind Corrie's fluttering lashes and sweet smile. Her interest was piqued just as his was. He decided to stay out of Jules and Corrie's way, and simply listen.

"You wouldn't believe me if I told you," Larry said with a knowing grin. Corrie rested her chin on her hand.

"Try me."

"It was a month ago, now," Larry began. He settled into his seat, clearly enjoying his captive audience. "You understand I'm licensed for groundfish. Any bycatch, anything not halibut, hake, cod, goes back to the sea. Well, we ran out the nets for the last haul of the day. Sonny was at the tiller, and my boy Trent was manning the winch, so that left me to handle the nets. When they dumped into the hold, there was something different there."

"What was it?" Corrie breathed. Jules caught Zeb's eye and grinned at Corrie's antics.

"A fish that shined like a big old rainbow. About this long." Larry held up his hands a shoulder-length apart. "But that wasn't the strangest part. That fish, it had a horn."

"Come on, Larry," Jules said. "You expect us to believe that?"

"It's the God's honest truth," Larry said. He slapped his palm on the table for emphasis. "That fish had a horn. I nabbed the slippery devil—almost gored me with its pointer—and put it in a cooler. I wanted to show the boys."

"I believe you, Larry." Jules put a hand on Larry's shoulder and stood up. "Thousands wouldn't, but I do. Now, if you'll excuse me, I need to visit the little boys' room."

Jules wandered off, and Corrie scooted her chair closer.

"What did you do next?"

"Well, I had touched the slimy thing, right, then I put a finger in my mouth by accident. Next thing I know, I'm tripping balls." Larry's eyes grew wide and he spread his hands around his face for effect. "Tripping absolute fucking balls. Pardon my French, my dear." Larry patted Corrie's hand, and she smiled indulgently.

"What, it had a drug-like effect?" Zeb leaned into the table again in fascination. His mother had never mentioned that little fact. Had she not known, or had she deemed it an unsuitable topic for a child? "How long did it last?"

"A half hour, maybe?" Larry took a deep draft of his beer with a satisfied smack. "It was unreal. Never had anything like it, and I dabbled in my younger years. All the boys tried some, same thing. I sold the fish to a friend of a friend—he wanted to keep the fish in a tank, bottle up the slime to sell."

"That's fascinating," Corrie said. "I wonder what sort of bait would attract one?"

It was an excellent question, but Zeb had been hoping to hear more about the strange effects. It was unexpected information, and every little bit helped to enlighten his mysteries.

"You don't want to play around with that junk," Larry told Corrie with a paternal chuckle, and she dipped her head. "Pretty thing like you, shouldn't get into that sort of mess."

"I was just curious." Corrie pouted then smiled. "Why hasn't anyone caught one before?"

"Ha! You wouldn't believe it. I was eating, looking at the fish, and dropped some in the cooler. That fish gobbled it up like a cat on catnip."

"What was it?"

"A bit of—" Larry smacked his forehead and looked contrite. "Sorry, Matt paid me good money not to say. I don't want to pay him back." He guffawed. "I already spent it!"

A flash of annoyance crossed Corrie's face. Zeb's jaw

117

tightened. Larry knew what bait to use to attract a strolia, and he wouldn't tell them? Corrie's eyes flickered to Zeb, and she gave him an expectant look. It took Zeb a moment to realize she was hinting for him to offer Larry money to talk. His eyes widened. Corrie thought he was rolling in cash, which was far from the truth. But could he afford not to find out?

"What'll it take to loosen your tongue?" Zeb said. "Surely this Matt guy would understand if you'd drunk too much." He pushed the beer closer to Larry. "You might not even remember saying anything."

Larry shook his head.

"Sorry, friends, but my word is my bond. Besides, Matt Nielsen is one big son of a gun. Don't want to get on his bad side, you know what I'm saying?" He stood up with a groan. "Thanks for the drink, folks. You enjoy your night."

Larry ambled off to the bar. Corrie looked at Zeb.

"Damn it! He knows how to catch one."

"And he won't tell us." Zeb tried to remain calm, but his chest was so tight he could hardly breathe. "We were so close."

"At least we know it's attracted to human food. That narrows it down—sort of."

"Speaking of food, where's Jules?" Krista stood in front of their table. "I thought we were getting dinner here."

"I'll find him," Zeb said. He'd lost his appetite. The frustration of coming so close to information but not getting it gnawed at his stomach. To his surprise, Corrie stood with him.

"I'll come too."

"Come on," Krista said with a wave to the door. "The village idiot was outside, last I saw."

JULES

"It's great stuff," the man said. Jules couldn't remember his name, although he'd introduced himself only minutes before. He was small and wiry, with a high-pitched voice. "You won't regret it. No aftereffects, either. Just good, clean fun." The man winked and Jules laughed.

"What the hell, I'll bite. Why's it so cheap?"

"Producer's just getting started, trying to find out demand. Price will go up soon. Try it now while you can afford it."

Jules dug into his pocket for his wallet. It was light—Zeb wouldn't pay him until after the week was done—but there was enough for one hit. He slid out a bill and handed it to the man, who pocketed it and gave Jules a tiny parcel of twisted wax paper.

"Eat the cracker inside—it's got the stuff on it. Tastes horrible, so down the hatch in one."

Jules nodded. The man saluted him and walked away, pulling a gray hoodie over his head. Jules untwisted the paper. Inside was a saltine cracker, slightly discolored but dry. Jules grimaced, then he shrugged and popped the cracker in his mouth. The novelty of the drug attracted him—he'd tried other substances in the past, for kicks, but this was entirely new, according to the seller—and he didn't see any reason why not to do it. The price was right, and he didn't have to do any work until tomorrow. It wasn't as if what he did would matter to anyone.

"There you are," Krista's strident voice called out. Jules swallowed the cracker and turned around. His three boat mates walked toward him, and he mustered an easy grin.

"Hi, all. Find out more about your fish?"

"A bit," Zeb said, his calm face stoic as usual, although traces of frustration marked his mouth for Jules' experienced eyes to see. "Tell you more on the boat."

119

"Come on, we're hungry." Krista waved at him impatiently, and Jules slowed his approach to annoy her. "What were you doing out here, anyway?"

"Trying new things. Hey, maybe I should get that dealer back here. You could stand to loosen up, Krista."

"Dealer?" Zeb looked worried. Jules did his best, but Krista's uptight influence infected Zeb from time to time.

"Yeah, hot new product on the market. Still new, so it's cheap enough that even I can afford it. Good times for half an hour, and no aftereffects. What's not to love?" Jules continued toward the pub's entrance. "Let's order."

The pub jumped to the left. He stumbled when the ground buckled to account for the pub's movement.

"Jules?" Zeb grabbed his arm. Alarm colored his voice. "What's happening?"

"Damn pub moved on me," Jules muttered. "Tell it to stay still."

Corrie gave a murmur of consternation, but Jules only had eyes for the enormous humpback whale lounging behind the pub. It was a lurid purple with blue eyes like crystals and five horns surrounding its upper lip.

"Why does it have five horns?" Jules said. "Seems excessive. A waste of good horn, if you ask me."

This struck him as quite witty, and he started to laugh. Zeb whirled him around until they were face to face. His pale eyes stared into Jules' own.

"What did you take?"

"Told you, it's new." Jules' eyes widened and he clutched Zeb's shoulders to throw him to the ground. "Watch out! That whale is moving this way!"

The ground was no better. From nowhere, rivers of herring poured in between him and Zeb. The smell of rotting fish was intense, and Jules threw his arms up as a shield. All his muscles felt hot. Then, everything started to jitter, but he wasn't sure if it was the world or himself. The whale rolled

120

over the pub, and a large flipper pinned Jules' legs and torso. He flailed wildly, but the flipper was far too heavy. The whale rolled further, and then Jules didn't know anything, anymore.

CORRIE

Zeb lifted the shuddering Jules around his torso. Krista grabbed Jules' legs, but one kicked out of her grasp. Corrie shook herself out of her shock and ran to help. She and Krista each gripped a leg firmly and the three of them hauled Jules away from the staring patrons of the pub.

"To the dinghy," Zeb panted. "There's no clinic on this island. If he keeps this up, it'll be quicker to take him to the nearest hospital if we're on the boat already."

Corrie nodded and looked at Jules. His face was covered in a sheen of sweat, and his eyes darted wildly to look at things that only he could see. She shuddered at the memories his actions dredged up and clenched Jules' spasming leg more securely.

At the dinghy, she did her best to lower his leg into the little vessel. Krista threw hers in unceremoniously and leaped to the motor, but Zeb carefully laid Jules' body against the hull and tucked a life jacket under his swinging head. The motor roared to life and they zoomed away from the dock. Corrie hugged herself against the cool night air and counted backward from one hundred to distract herself. When they were at the boat, she could do things to help, keep busy. In the dinghy, there was only the spasming Jules and her thoughts. She pushed the image of a body lying on a tiled bathroom floor, pale and unmoving, out of her head and focused on counting.

At the boat, Zeb jumped out and moved the winch to haul up the boat. Krista attached the dinghy and she and Corrie climbed out. Jules stayed in the bottom until the dinghy was in place on the deck, then Zeb gently put him in a fireman's carry and took him to their shared cabin. Corrie rushed into the galley and found a container and towel then raced to the cabin. Zeb was tucking Jules into the bottom bunk when she burst in.

"Here are some things he might need," she said. "How is he?"

"Calming," Zeb said with a finger on Jules' wrist. "And his heartrate and breathing are strong. I think he'll be okay. Whatever he took seems to be wearing off already." He looked at the items in Corrie's hands. "Good thinking. You do this often, do you?"

He clearly meant the comment in jest, despite his usual deadpan delivery, but Corrie flushed. The truth was closer that Zeb realized. She put the container and towel on the floor beside the bunk.

"It might come in handy." She retreated before Zeb could probe further and joined Krista in the galley.

"What an idiot," Krista grumbled. "Seriously, he never thinks about consequences. Never thinks, actually. He's been like that as long as I've known him. It doesn't surprise me that he found some experimental drug and then thought, 'Yes, that sounds like a good idea.' Typical, really."

"Stop it, Krista," Zeb said from the doorway. "Keep your toxic comments to yourself."

"I'm not the one with toxins," she said, but she turned to open the fridge. "If we're not en route to the hospital, I'm getting those cold cuts out. I'm starving."

Corrie snuck a glance at Zeb. He looked worried and tired. Then he glanced at her.

"Do you think this has anything to do with the fish?"

Understanding lit up Corrie's brain. The drug-like effect that Larry had described—he said it lasted for half an hour and was like an acid trip. Jules' ravings had certainly sounded similar.

"Do you think they're producing it commercially already?" she whispered. "Larry said it had only been a month."

"What are you two talking about?" Krista demanded, her

hands busy making a sandwich.

Zeb filled her in on Larry's story. Krista continued assembling her sandwich, but her measured movements and tilted head told Corrie that she was listening intently.

"And he sold the fish to someone who wanted to 'bottle it up.' Make some money off it, I guess. Someone named Matt Nielsen."

"Matt Nielsen?" Krista whipped around and stared at Zeb. "That's what he said?"

"Yeah," Zeb said, looking confused. "You know him?"

"Yeah, I know him," Krista said darkly. "He's my friend Erika's brother. Erika moved to Campbell River to live with her aunt for our last year of high school. He's a tool—Erika never had good things to say about him. I thought he was out of the country."

A presence at the door made Corrie jump, but it was only Jules. He had a blanket around his shoulders. His pale face attempted to smile at them all, but it was clearly forced and didn't last.

"Hi," he croaked.

Zeb looked him over critically. When he appeared satisfied that Jules wasn't about to keel over, he pushed his friend's shoulder gently.

"What the hell were you thinking?" Zeb shook his head. "Seriously, man, one day it won't be a good time, and you won't spring back from it."

"It wasn't a good time now," Jules said with a shudder. "Horrible visions. Crazy wild, I guess, but too much for me. Too vivid."

"It is a new drug," Corrie said. "Maybe it reacts differently to different people. Or maybe it mixed adversely with the alcohol in your system."

Jules nodded then looked at Zeb, who stared at him with his arms crossed.

"It doesn't matter," Jules said. He gave a nonchalant

shrug. "Good trip, bad trip, life goes on."

"If you're lucky," said Zeb.

"Then that's the way the cookie crumbles."

Zeb gave his friend an incredulous stare. Corrie bit her lip. What did Jules mean? Before Zeb could follow up, Krista pitched in with a change in topic.

"So, let me sum this up for those of us who were writhing around on their bunks. Matt Nielsen bought a unicorn fish off a fisherman and knows what bait to use to catch more. He's trying to collect a substance from this fish to sell and is so far successful. Does that about cover it?"

"This unicorn fish, this potentially new species of fish, never before documented by science, is being exploited to make street drugs?" Corrie felt her anger rising. "There might only be one school of these fish in the entire world, and they're already being harvested without knowing anything about them. It's criminal."

"And it's Matt Nielsen," Krista added. "He's a bastard. Take him down, I say."

"We need to find a unicorn fish," Corrie said. Deep in her gut she felt the tragedy of losing a new species before it had been found. It wouldn't be the first time in human history. "We need to document it, learn about it, save it. Before it's too late and they're all gone."

Everyone stared at Zeb. He paused for a moment, thinking.

"So," he said at last. "We need to test bait to catch a st— unicorn fish. We need to find Matt Nielsen and stop him, somehow. And we need to keep doing your science, Corrie. Does that sound right?"

Corrie had almost forgotten her anemones in the uproar. She nodded emphatically.

"Yes, yes, and yes," she said.

"I'm in," said Krista. "For the next five days, anyway. Then it's back to the real world, and the weird fish will have to fend for themselves." She stared at Zeb, who looked away from his sister's meaningful glare.

"Let's do it," said Jules. "Might as well. But how do we figure out the bait?"

"It's some sort of food," Zeb said. "Something that fisherman Larry likes to eat. Tomorrow, we'll go grocery shopping and try a bit of everything."

ZEBALLOS

Jules went to bed without eating. Zeb, Corrie, and Krista raided the fridge and pulled together enough bread, cheese, and meat to satisfy before they turned in. Zeb hardly spoke. He was consumed with thoughts of the unknown Matt Nielsen collecting strolias and plans to capture one of his own. Krista tried to draw him out once or twice, and it wasn't until Corrie gave him a concerned look before heading to bed that he realized his sister had been trying to shelter him from Corrie's curiosity over his silence.

Jules was asleep when he slid into his bunk. Zeb thought he would be tossing and turning all night, but when the sun streamed in the tiny window at daylight, he sat up with a start. Jules was already gone, so he dressed and headed to the galley. Today, they would discover what strolias were attracted to. Today, they would catch one. He had a good feeling about today.

"You're up already," he said to Jules, who was flipping pancakes in the galley. Jules bent down to rummage in the fridge for milk.

"I figured making breakfast was the least I could do after last night. Besides, it is what you're paying me for. Here, take this to the table."

Jules handed Zeb a plate with a stack of pancakes teetering haphazardly on it. Zeb hesitated.

"You feeling okay?"

Jules swallowed, then shot Zeb a grin.

"Yeah, sure. I bounce back from everything."

"Okay."

Zeb hovered for a moment more, but there didn't seem to be anything else to say, so he carried on to the table with his plate. Moments later, Corrie wandered in, a huge yawn splitting her face.

"When's the first station?" She sank onto the bench and eyed the pancakes with appreciation.

"That's up to you," said Zeb. He pulled out a chart of the area and spread it in front of Corrie. He pointed at a location. "We're here, in this bay. We could do the two stations you had planned today, here and here. Or, we could go to the grocery store in Nodales." He pointed at the chart again. "And pick up supplies for catching our fish. Then we could do one of your stations in the afternoon."

Corrie's eyes gleamed.

"Well, yeah. Let's do it. I really need to take those samples, but the unicorn fish…" She studied the chart for a moment. "Could we do my second station in the evening? Is that crazy? I don't mind working into the night, if you're okay with diving after dinner."

Zeb was impressed by her dedication. As far as he was concerned, he was working this week, twenty-four hours a day. And if something he could do would further his hunt for strolias, he was on board.

"Not crazy at all," he assured her. "We'll do it."

Zeb loaded a plate with pancakes and carried it to the door. He was already composing a shopping list. What sort of hand food would someone be eating while watching a fish?

"If you see Krista, tell her I'm hauling anchor."

By the time Zeb had started the engine and taken up the anchor, Krista had finished her breakfast and come into the wheelhouse. She took the wheel while Zeb prepared the dinghy. Fifteen minutes later, they launched the little boat, and he and Corrie zoomed to a distant dock on the beachfront of a town.

"What are we looking for, do you think?" Corrie said as he held the door open for her at a corner grocery store.

"I have no idea. Handheld foods, something that might fall or drip." He held out his hands helplessly. "Anything that looks reasonable. I'll get a basket."

128

"Definitely lots of fishy stuff," Corrie said as they went down the canned food aisle. She threw in cans of tuna and salmon. Her nose wrinkled in thought at a jar of anchovy paste, then she shrugged and tossed it in the basket. "It only stands to reason. Smelly food, too—it would be the most likely to attract fish in water."

"Like this?" Zeb held up a jar of sauerkraut. "Kind of a long shot."

"Worth a try. Who knows, maybe Larry really loves peanut butter and pickle sandwiches."

"Or hardboiled eggs wrapped in cabbage."

Corrie laughed, a delicate sound that made the corners of Zeb's mouth turn up. They spent the next half hour finding the smelliest and most ludicrous snack foods they could think of. When Zeb presented the basket of groceries to the cashier, she raised an eyebrow.

"Quite the feast you've got there," she said.

"My Polish-Korean grandmother swears by kimchi over perogies," Corrie said with a straight face. Zeb coughed to cover his surprised snort of humor. Corrie gave him a triumphant look. Zeb found out why when they left the store.

"I made you laugh," she said with a smug smile. "It's almost an impossible task."

Zeb glanced at her in confusion. Did he really seem that dull to her?

"What, you think I don't have a sense of humor?"

"Well, it doesn't come out much if you do." Corrie swung her grocery bag as they walked on the side of the road toward the dock. "Don't worry about it. You look as though you have a lot on your mind. I'm sure you're a riot at parties." She glanced at him with a half-smile to tell him she was teasing. Zeb wasn't sure what to think. He knew he was quiet, but he'd never been told he was dull. Anger and frustration over his father's secrets, combined with the stress of money and keeping secrets on the boat, must have made

129

him more closed-off than usual.

"It's been a tough few months since my dad died," he said after a moment. Corrie looked contrite.

"Jeez, I forgot about that. I'm sorry."

Corrie was quiet for a few uncharacteristic moments. Zeb tried to find something to fill the silence. He didn't want Corrie to think he lacked conversation skills as well as being humorless.

"Are you getting enough data for your science project?" he asked. "Since we've been chasing unicorn fish, I mean. I hope it's not getting in the way of your work."

Corrie sighed. Zeb hoped she didn't take his words too seriously. He was trying to chat with the only topic that came to mind, not convince her to stop looking for strolias. He held his breath until she spoke.

"I know, I should focus more on my project. But it's so amazing to think how close we are to finding one. I would never forgive myself if I didn't try. My thesis is important, sure, but I've been chasing legends since I was ten years old. This is more than a passing interest for me."

Zeb let out his breath. That was what he wanted to hear.

"I'll work late, work hard," she continued. "It's only a week. I can push through and do it all. Can you imagine if we actually catch a unicorn fish? What that would do for my career? Forget validating my personal beliefs. It could *make* me, career-wise. I can't even imagine the repercussions to the scientific community with this discovery."

Zeb frowned. That was an angle he hadn't considered. Of course, he knew that bringing someone else into hunting legends was risky for him. He hadn't thought through what Corrie would do with the information she might find. What would it mean, to him or to the legends he so desperately searched for, if their secrets were exposed to the world? He didn't have an answer to that.

"Let's find one first," he said.

CORRIE

Zeb was quiet, as usual, in the dinghy on the way back to the boat. Sunlight made his already pale hair almost white against his deeply tanned skin. Corrie would have paid good money to see pictures of his parents—she couldn't imagine a more unlikely combination of features than what Zeb sported. Suddenly, she ached to be at home with her roommates for a round of gossiping. There was so much fodder here to work with, and no one to share with. Jules was good for a chat, sure, but Zeb was closed off and Krista hated her, for some undisclosed reason but-totally-not-Corrie's fault, according to Zeb.

Corrie flipped her braid off her shoulder defiantly. It didn't matter. She had a mission, and she would execute it. Two missions, in fact. Capture and study a unicorn fish and get the best damn samples she could for her metabolomics project. She would set herself up for the thesis of the year. Mara would be infuriated if Corrie published more papers from her project than she did. With that happy thought, Corrie started to talk to Zeb again.

"What's the plan with the bait? How are we going to catch these sneaky little devils?"

"Two ideas," Zeb said, scanning for logs ahead. "Set up a bunch at a cave with the net trap, and tow a few fishing lines off the back of the boat. We'll find a cave close to your next station. I can set it up while you're doing the bottles with Jules."

"Awesome," said Corrie. "Let's do it. And if we have leftover ground beef from the bait, maybe I can get Jules to make spaghetti. My grandma, while she wasn't Polish-Korean, still made mean meatballs. I bet I can remember the recipe. Jules could probably make it better than grandma, although she'd roll over in her grave if she heard me say that.

She wasn't the greatest cook, and Jules is much better. Seriously, does he work in a restaurant? So good. Grandma was from France, actually, so I have no idea where she learned how to make spaghetti…"

Corrie knew she was rambling, but Zeb was so quiet that she felt she had to fill the void. She couldn't tell if he was listening to her or whether he had zoned out minutes ago and was nodding to the beat of his own inner music. Whatever. It soothed her to talk, to have something fill the silence, and if Zeb had a problem with that, he could pitch in with conversation sometime.

When they reached the boat a few minutes later, Jules helped winch up the dinghy. Krista made the engine roar to life, and they were off. The trip wasn't far, and Corrie had barely enough time to prepare her bottles and collection bags before the engine noise slowed to a dull grumble and Jules' voice called her from the aft deck.

"It's anemone time!"

Suit back on, equipment checked, mask in place—Corrie was beginning to feel comfortable with the routine of sampling. The nerves of the first day had faded into confident movements and steady breathing. She nodded at Zeb then fell backward into the water. The shock of cold seawater on her face gave her an instant headache, as always, but she fought through the sensation, and it passed as the water between her neoprene hood and her head warmed up. Waves splashed her about, so she waited only until Zeb entered the water with a mighty splash and gave her the okay signal before descending. The air might be constrictive and the visibility murky, but at least waves weren't pummeling her about.

She collected her samples quickly and efficiently, pausing only for a moment to enjoy the bright yellow of a lemon nudibranch on a rock nearby. Zeb floated behind her, moving with minimal strokes of his feet and maintaining perfect buoyancy. She envied him that—her mastery of buoyancy left something to be desired, but she fumbled through well enough—although he did wear a wetsuit instead of a dry suit, which was supposed to be easier. That must be it.

Samples collected, she turned for the boat again, but realized she was helplessly lost. She checked her compass, but she'd strayed far enough off her initial line in search of the perfect clump of anemones that she doubted its usefulness. She put her hands up in a shrug in Zeb's direction and pointed at her compass. Without a flicker of worry, Zeb motioned for her to follow him. They tracked a straight line directly to the shadow of the boat that lay on the ocean floor, and Corrie marveled at Zeb's insanely accurate sense of direction.

When they were back on the boat and had removed their suits, Zeb's face changed from the serenity of underwater to a grimace of discomfort.

"Are you feeling okay?" Corrie asked. "You look a little funny."

"Fine, thanks." He tried for a smile, but it didn't come out right on his pained expression. "I'll put the bait in the cave while you're doing the bottles. Be back in a minute."

Before Corrie could say another word, he fled to the winch controls and swung the dinghy out into the water.

"Ready?" said Jules. He held a collection bottle out to Corrie. She shook her head to clear it and reached out to grab the bottle.

"Sure thing."

ZEBALLOS

Zeb leaped into the dinghy and tore off toward a nearby cave. Maybe if he went fast enough, the itching on his skin would fade. Zeb knew better, but hope was a strangely persistent beast.

He strung a net across the mouth of the cave then reached out to attach the bag he had prepared during their trip here. It was filled with a little bit of everything they had bought, mashed together for optimum scent leakage. Surely, one of the items would work. Zeb plunged his hands into the seawater to tie the bag to the other side of the trap. He moaned at the touch of water on his hands, and the itching on the rest of his body intensified. The dive had once again enflamed him, given him a taste of a swim without providing the real joys of being in the water. His body cried that it wasn't enough. Ruthlessly, he ignored it and finished tying a knot, then took his hands out of the water. He opened the throttle on the engine with a grim set to his mouth. He could handle it. This was no time to surrender. Corrie would be done her collection soon, and they would steam away to the next station. There was no time for a swim. His body would simply have to deal with it.

By the time he reached the boat, his skin was on fire with longing for cool saltiness to caress it. He climbed aboard and handled the winch operations with shaking fingers. Corrie came around and greeted him.

"Bottles all done! I'm ready to go anytime."

"Great," he forced out through clenched teeth. An idea popped into his head. "I need to check something before we go. Engine. Shouldn't take long. You have lab work to do?"

"Do I ever," Corrie said with a roll of her eyes. "It'll take me a month of Sundays to get through. No worries, take your time. It's not far to the next station, is it?"

134

"No, not at all," he assured her without remembering where they were going next. "I'll be as quick as I can."

Corrie disappeared into the lab and Zeb raced to grab his flippers from behind the life ring. He paused only to poke his head into the wheelhouse.

"Corrie's done, but don't go yet. I need a minute."

"A minute for what?" Krista's eyes narrowed. "Zeb, come on. Once is a risk. Twice is just stupid. Corrie could come around and see you at any minute. What reason would you have for swimming without a wetsuit in this weather? It's hardly summer temperatures."

"She won't see, it's fine." At his sister's disbelieving eyes, he burst out, "I can't take it. Diving without a proper swim is driving me crazy. I can't feel anything down there in that suit, and I can't hear with the bubbles. It's torture."

Krista gazed at him for a moment then sighed.

"Go on. But make it quick."

Zeb's shirt was off and he was halfway to the bow before Krista finished her sentence. He jumped out of his pants, leaving only his swimsuit on, and fitted on his flippers. With a graceful dive, he slid into the water with barely a ripple.

Instantly, the itching fire on his skin faded into memory. He rolled around and around as he descended, reveling in the brush of cool water over his bare skin. Although he swam frequently in his life, this fiery need for it daily was unusual. The diving must have been causing it, as he told Krista, aggravating him beyond endurance.

Now, he was calm and centered. He waved a hand over a scallop on the rocky bottom, and it started to swim, clapping its shells together to shoot jets of water and scoot over the ocean floor. Zeb smiled widely. He would have laughed if he hadn't been holding his breath. He rolled again, just for the fun of it.

What about the cave? It was close enough for him to swim to. He could check the bait before they left. He kicked, thrusting his body forward with powerful strokes in an unerring straight line to the cave, the currents on his body directing him true.

When he was near, the pattern of waves rolling above his head like frothy mirrors, he paused and looked around. No sign of any strolias. A memory came to Zeb, floating from the deeper recesses of his mind, back from a happier time when his mother had been alive. The two of them underwater, his mother's long, pale hair floating like seaweed in the current. His mother opening her mouth and producing a clicking sound with her tongue. A school of perch coming to investigate.

Zeb opened his mouth but kept his tongue in position to block his airway. He clucked his tongue experimentally. A series of clicks emerged. Encouraged, he clicked a half-remembered pattern. A black-eyed goby rose from the seaweed to eye him beadily. He tried for another minute, but no strolias loomed out of the murky waters. He clicked until an ache in his chest reminded him of his need for air. He swam toward the boat, disappointed but still hopeful. They had only just put out the new bait. Maybe, with a little time, they would trap a strolia. And then, he could begin to unravel the mysteries of his life.

KRISTA

Krista made Jules take the wheel when he finished with Corrie's samples, and she was now waiting on the port side for Zeb to surface. One eye was on the water, and one was on Corrie in the lab. Krista regretted letting Zeb dive in. Not that she had much say over anything Zeb did—he was his own man and didn't take heed of his older sister's warnings, more's the pity. Sometimes, she missed the days when he was small enough to put in a headlock until he surrendered. He was obstinate, that was certain.

Although, today was different. He hadn't simply brushed off her concerns about swimming with Corrie on board. No, he was quite desperate to get in the water again, with an almost manic glint in his eyes. It was unnerving. That was why she had capitulated, not because she thought it was a sensible idea. Zeb's distraction has scared her. It was so unlike him. He was always calm, too calm, really—cold water to Krista's hot fire. What would have happened had Zeb been restrained, not allowed to get in the water? Would his desire fade eventually, or would he grow even more desperate? Krista crossed her arms to ward off the uncomfortable thoughts.

Zeb finally surfaced right next to the boat. Krista leaned over.

"Hey Krista, do you know when lunch is?" Corrie said behind her. Krista froze. "I'm trying to time my analysis to fit eating in. It's a crime to let Jules' food get cold."

Krista whirled around. Corrie's focus was on her hands stripping off her gloves, but in a moment, she would look up. Krista waved her hand frantically at Zeb and hoped he would take the hint.

"I don't know," she said, her voice coming out steadily despite the thumping of her heart. "Better go ask. He's in the wheelhouse."

Corrie joined her at the railing. Krista chanced a glance at the ocean, but nothing marred the rolling surface except for two seagulls bobbing a few boat lengths distant.

"Is Zeb still fixing the engine?" Corrie asked. "I wanted to talk to him about our next station."

"Yes, right. I'll send him your way when he's done. Shouldn't be much longer now." Krista waited, her breath shallow. Corrie gazed at the waves for a few long moments.

"Okay, thanks. See you later." Corrie turned and walked to the wheelhouse. Once she had disappeared inside, Krista grabbed a shackle from the deck floor and dropped it overboard.

A moment later, Zeb emerged, shackle in hand. Krista waved him over.

"Hurry up," she hissed. "She'll be back any minute."

She lowered the ladder as quietly as she could, and her dripping brother clambered up it. He helped her haul the ladder to the deck, then walked quickly to the aft deck to find his towel. Krista followed him and smacked his head.

"Ouch!" Zeb rubbed the spot and glared at her. "What was that for?"

"You were being an idiot," Krista said. She was angry at him for being so foolish, yes, but her anger was easier to unleash than her fear. "What if Corrie had seen? She almost did, you know."

"And what would happen if she did?" he demanded. "She would think I was weird, swimming in this water, but nothing I couldn't explain."

"And when you didn't surface for ten minutes? When she was calling for the coast guard to rescue you, and we were left to explain that you were just fine? What then?"

Zeb stared at her. There was no response to that, and he knew it. She crossed her arms.

"I don't know what the rush was all about," she said. "But

138

you have to figure it out. There are four more days of this, eight or ten stations left. The odds are against you if you keep this up."

Zeb looked away. His eyes were troubled but held none of the manic tension of earlier.

"I don't know what's going on," he said. "It was too much, being in the water but not feeling it. Like my body wasn't getting what I had promised it. Scuba diving has always bugged me, but the feeling has never been that strong before."

"Do what you need to do, but be smart about it. Make a plan." Krista was starting to rethink this whole trip, not that she hadn't been against it from the start. "I still don't think it's wise getting Corrie involved in all this. I know she's in too deep, now, but still." She didn't even know what she was protesting, anymore. She only knew the nagging doubt in her gut wouldn't let her relax, enjoy Corrie's company, or let her guard down. She didn't have an answer, but she knew allowing Zeb to risk himself like this wasn't it.

"Yes, she is." Zeb didn't elaborate. They both knew the other's stance, and neither had budged. He changed the topic. "What do you think of the strolias?"

"You really think that's what they are?" Krista was unconvinced the unicorn fish were the strolias from her stepmother Clicker's stories, but they were odd. She supposed Clicker's tales had to have come from somewhere. It didn't mean that the rest of them were true. "I don't know, Zeb. They're weird, that's for sure. I don't know if they are what you hope they are."

She didn't want to encourage him at all. He and Corrie were feeding off each other's fascination—they didn't need help. Jules was no good, either. Although not as curious as the other two, he didn't speak against it.

"They are." Zeb resumed his toweling dry with a dismissive posture. Krista's hackles rose at his indifference to

139

facts.

"We need to fill up with gas soon," she said. "It's expensive out here, especially without a charter group paying us. Lucky there are only four days left before Corrie leaves and we can go back to shore."

"I'm not stopping until I catch a strolia," he said with an air of finality.

"You said—"

"I said I'd stop at the end of summer. But that was before I saw one. This is actual proof that my mum's stories are real. This is the closest I've ever been to finding out what Dad was hiding from me."

"You promised that you'd get your shit together in the fall." Krista was fuming now, her hands balled into fists. Her stupid little brother was throwing his future away on a whim. If these secrets were so well-kept, maybe he'd be better off leaving them alone. Leave the past in the past, she always said.

"How can you ask me to stop now?" Zeb's eyes flashed with anger of his own. "I need to know. You don't understand."

"You're right. I don't." She stepped forward and poked him on his bare chest with a taut finger. "You're forgetting reality while you're chasing myths. The money won't last forever, and then you'll have nothing."

She spun around and stormed down the side of the boat, wishing that they weren't stuck on fifty feet of vessel in the middle of the ocean. She wanted to put far more distance between them.

Krista was too mad at Zeb to speak to him for the rest of the day beyond necessities. She rarely bothered chatting to

140

Jules, and Corrie was part and parcel of Zeb's whole warped reality, so when Krista wasn't helping with sampling efforts or driving the boat, she kept to herself. It was no mean feat on a vessel the size of the *Clicker*, but Krista was nothing if not ingenious. She took her dinner to the bow and ate a solitary meal in the light of the setting sun.

By morning, Krista had almost forgiven Zeb for being so stupid. He couldn't help it, really. That was how he was made. That's why Clicker had tasked her with looking after him. Even at age eight, Zeb's foolhardiness must have been apparent, even to his mother.

Krista had no intention of letting Zeb know he was off the hook, though.

"Good morning," Zeb said when he entered the wheelhouse. Krista, at the wheel already and driving to their next station, merely grunted without taking her eyes off the water. Zeb shrugged. "Here are the coordinates. Let us know when we're there."

He turned, but before he could leave, Krista spoke.

"Do you have a plan? For after sampling with Corrie?"

Zeb paused.

"Dad had that old rope ladder stashed in the engine room," he said to the door. "I'll put that over the bow and jump in as soon as Corrie starts her water collection with Jules."

He left without waiting for a response. Krista's anger flared again. Well, if he didn't want any advice, he wouldn't get any. It was a fine enough plan, she supposed. More holes than a net, but that was all they had to work with.

A half hour later saw them passing Harwood Island where Zeb had set up a trap in a cave yesterday. Krista slowed. Zeb would be sure to want to check it if they were passing. A boat crept into view around the tip of the island. Krista narrowed her eyes in thought. Was that the *Defiance*? Her old high school friend Erika's family used to own it. Still did, if she

141

remembered correctly, although it wasn't the season for herring, nor the place. That could only mean…

"Zeb," she called out on the intercom radio. "Get up here." She pulled at the wheel and pointed the bow directly at the *Defiance*.

Zeb swung into the cabin a moment later.

"What are you doing?" he said. "Are we stopping to check the trap?"

"Look." Krista pointed at the boat. "That's the boat of Matt Nielsen's family. What do you bet he's here, catching unicorn fish for his new drug empire?"

Zeb stared at her and then at the boat.

"What are you planning?" he said slowly.

"Telling him to back off." She grinned, although there was no humor in the expression. "Don't worry, little brother. Let me do the talking."

When she pulled the *Clicker* alongside the *Defiance*, Matt came around the cabin to find out what was going on. Krista motioned Zeb to take the wheel and strode to the deck.

"Matt Nielsen!" she shouted across the water, her strong voice carrying easily. "Long time, no see."

"Krista Artino?" he said with a frown. "I thought you were living in Vancouver."

"And I thought you were sailing the seven seas. But you're not doing that anymore, are you?" Krista's eyes glanced around the deck of his boat, but there was nothing suspicious in sight. Still, they knew what he was up to. "What are you doing with the horned fish?"

Matt's body stiffened and his eyes widened. Krista took a wider stance in triumph. That was confirmation if she'd ever seen it.

"I don't know what you're talking about," he said.

"Sure, you don't. You know my friend here almost died last night because of your new drug?" Krista waved at the stern where she assumed Jules was. It was a stretch to say he

142

almost died, and an even further stretch to say that they were friends, but it sounded good out loud. Matt's face darkened.

"Are you accusing me of something?"

"What are you doing here, if not catching those mutant fish?" she said. "Do you even know anything about them? They could be radioactive, for all you know."

"I don't have to listen to this," Matt said. He started to turn.

"We're not going to let this go," she shouted. "We'll expose you. Gather as much evidence as we need. We will stop you."

Matt's attempt at calm exploded, and his face contorted with anger.

"Back off, bitch. You have nothing, and you know nothing. If you try anything, I will make you pay."

"Is that a threat?"

"Glad you're so perceptive. Now get out of my sight before I do something you'll regret."

"Krista," Zeb called from the wheelhouse. "We're leaving now."

The engine kicked into gear, and the *Clicker* started to move. Krista gave Matt the finger before turning away in disgust. What a lowlife. He'd gone even further downhill since his youth, that was apparent. And Erika was such a decent person.

Jules and Corrie followed her into the wheelhouse. It was too small for four people, but they squeezed in all the same. Zeb's face at the wheel was set in a worried frown.

"What the hell was that about, Krista?" he said.

"What do you mean? I wanted to see if he was guilty, and he just about told us straight-up."

"I bet he's catching one right now," Jules said. "We're right near one of the caves we set a trap on."

"Then he has the correct bait on board." Zeb glanced at Krista, and her eyes widened. Did Zeb think he was going to

143

find out what it was? Krista shook her head at him, but he powered down the boat. "I wish we could find out what it was. But while we're here, we should check the trap. Jules and Corrie, do you want to have a look this time?"

Zeb caught Jules' eye, and after a moment's silent conversation, Jules said, "Sure. Come on, Corrie, let's go find ourselves a unicorn fish."

ZEBALLOS

Jules and Corrie had hardly roared away in the dinghy before Zeb stripped off his clothes to reveal his swim suit underneath. His breath came in a fast pant, and his skin tingled with anticipation of cool salt water gliding over it. His mind, however, fastened on the problem at hand—how would he find out what bait Matt was using?

"How are you going to do this?" Krista's voice echoed his own thoughts. "You're not going to climb aboard, are you?"

"If it comes to it," Zeb said. When he caught his sister's horrified gaze, he amended, "But it won't. His line is probably in the water. I can swim over there, check it out, and come back without anyone being the wiser."

"Well, hurry up," she said with a glance after the retreating dinghy. "The others won't be long."

Zeb grabbed his flippers out of their hiding place and slid them on his feet, then took a practiced dive off the railing of the boat.

The water welcomed him with an all-encompassing embrace. Zeb glided with sure kicks down, down, and toward the shore. Tiny currents touching his body told him where to go, and he angled himself directly toward the hulking vessel floating on the surface of the bay. A small reef shark drifted toward him in curiosity. When Zeb made the croaking noise of a large wolf eel like his mother had taught him, the shark wandered off. Zeb would normally have welcomed the company, but today he was on a mission. They had to know what the bait was.

A shadow darkened the green murk before him. Zeb slowed and looked around carefully. Visibility was low so near the surface, but his other senses worked just fine. He closed his eyes to get a better reading.

To his left, a faint tingle indicated a fishing line. It was almost too weak to notice, but Zeb had trained himself many years ago. That must be Matt's line. Zeb kicked slowly toward it, keeping a close watch on his senses to avoid entangling himself in the line.

Before long, a glint of nylon caught his eye. He dived down to find the hook. Deeper and deeper he swam, the light dim down here from so much algae in the water above.

Then he saw it. A medium-sized hook, suitable for salmon fishing, was nearly buried in a chunk of bait. Zeb swam closer to see what it was. His eyes widened.

It was a strip of dried jellyfish. Most wouldn't have recognized it, but Zeb was the only one he knew who enjoyed it. He would never have guessed that the strolias would like that best, nor that Larry made a habit of eating it for a snack. Krista always turned her nose up at the rubbery texture, and although Jules had tried it for the sake of experimentation, he had never asked Zeb for a bite again.

Zeb smiled. Here, at last, they had something to work with. He had lots of dried jellyfish in the galley, tucked in a back cupboard where it wouldn't get in Jules' way or offend Krista's sensibilities. Krista bought it for him, grudgingly, from Vancouver's Chinatown. They could try to fish with it now. Maybe, if they were lucky, they could have their very own strolia this afternoon. His heart nearly burst with excitement.

He looked at the bait again. Should he remove it so that Matt wouldn't catch a strolia today? No, he decided. The line would jerk and tug, no matter how carefully he pulled the jellyfish off, and Matt would be alerted. Zeb didn't feel like a hook in the finger today. It wouldn't be the first time.

But was there something else Zeb could do to foil the budding drug producer? His eye landed on the boat's propeller. He smiled widely then dived down to fetch a rock. His plan would merely inconvenience Matt, but it would be satisfying to thwart him in some way. As long as Matt didn't start the engine—and it was doubtful he would, with his fishing line in the water—then it was a risk-free endeavor.

Back underneath the *Clicker*, Zeb examined his senses for clues. There was no sign of the dinghy, which either meant that Corrie and Jules were still at the cave, or they were already on board. He surfaced near the bow, just in case.

Krista spotted him and waved him aboard.

"They're not back yet," she called. "Hurry up."

He swam to the ladder and climbed quickly aboard. Krista threw him a towel and he ducked into the cabin. A towel-down, especially of his wet hair, and a change of clothes, and Zeb was ready. Corrie wouldn't suspect a thing.

CORRIE

The trap was empty, not that Corrie had expected anything different. It was an experiment based on so few known parameters. Their assumptions about the unicorn fish liking caves were just that, assumptions, and they clearly hadn't found the correct bait that would draw them in. Not for the first time, Corrie wondered if they should look up Larry the fisherman again and try to wheedle the information out of him.

"Let's get out of here," said Jules when he dropped the net back in the water. "You have some real sciencing to do."

"You're right," said Corrie with a sigh. "That water won't collect itself."

They were almost at the *Clicker* when a motion on the *Defiance* caught Corrie's eye. Matt was on the deck, struggling with his fishing line.

"Jules! He's got one!"

Jules put the dinghy into neutral and they both watched with open mouths. Whatever was on the other end of the fishing line was putting up a good fight. Matt let the line run out, then he reeled it in slowly until a great tug dipped his rod toward the water and he let the line run free again.

"He's playing it like a salmon," Jules said in a hushed voice.

"Will it work?"

"Maybe. Time will tell."

Krista and Zeb leaned over the railing of the *Clicker* to watch. After three runs and three long, slow reels-in, Matt's expression changed from intense concentration to one of triumph. With a mighty yank, he pulled the fish out of the water.

A silvery, rainbow-gleaming fish soared through the air. It writhed and flopped ceaselessly, its horn winking in the

148

sunlight.

"Damn," Jules breathed. "There it is. In the flesh."

Matt directed the spasming fish toward a bucket on deck. When it wouldn't stop its movements, he whacked it against the side of his boat. It was stunned enough to slow its flopping.

Corrie realized she was clutching the side of the dinghy so hard it hurt.

"What the hell?" she gasped. "What was that for?"

"Not really necessary," Jules said with a disgusted look on his face. "If he was going to kill it, I guess it's not a big deal, but if he's planning to keep it in a tank and harvest the drug somehow, that was cruel."

Matt wrangled a lid on his bucket and disappeared into the cabin. Corrie felt sick, but she climbed out of the dinghy and helped bring it to the boat deck. When the dinghy was on board, she faced the others.

"We need to stop this guy," she said. She noted that Krista looked nauseated at Matt's antics but was trying to hide it. Zeb nodded.

"Yeah, we have to figure this out." He glanced at the *Defiance*. "You know, that boat has seen better days. Needs some serious servicing. I wonder if it will even start." He gave Krista and Jules a meaningful look. While Krista mostly managed to cover her reaction with a blank expression, Jules hid his mirth in a cough.

What were they laughing at? It was the last thing Corrie felt like doing. But if they didn't want to share, she wouldn't make them. She turned to walk into the lab—at least she was the ruler of her little domain—when a sputtering noise caught her attention. The *Defiance* was starting up, but it sounded rough. Then something clanked, and the motor went quiet.

"That doesn't sound healthy," Jules said with an attempt at nonchalance.

149

MATHIAS

Matt picked up his cooler and hauled it to the dock. The *Defiance* was all fixed up, thanks to a tow from the coast guard and a quick fix by a local mechanic. He'd paid an arm and a leg for the service, but he couldn't afford to wait. His horned fish had to get into a tank, and Krista and her self-righteous friends were sniffing around. He needed to get away from them and get back to work. Sea Salt wasn't going to extract itself.

Matt paused to take a deep breath of the salty air of the inlet. His grandfather's cabin was nestled at the base of a sheer cliff beside a deep cut that disappeared into darkness. The cabin was on a tiny slice of land beside the cut, but it rarely saw sun because of the steep walls of the cliff. His grandfather had bought the land decades ago for cheap, with the far-flung dream of creating a fishing resort one day. That day had never come, lost in the bottle where dreams go to die, but he had built a small cabin. Matt, his brothers, father, uncles, cousins, and grandfather took a yearly trip to the cabin to fish and get plastered, not necessarily in that order. The rest of the year, the cabin lay abandoned.

It was the perfect secret lab.

Matt hefted the cooler more securely in his arms and walked the few steps to the cabin's front door. It was so close to the water that it would have felt more exposed had the inlet not protected it from ocean conditions. His cousin Pete had taken to calling Matt's operation the lab, although Matt thought "aquarium" was a more apt name. He opened the wooden door, which creaked no matter how many cans of lubricant he sprayed on the hinges, and surveyed the scene. Six tanks bubbled on one side of the main room. Horned fish swam in slow circles in three of the tanks. Their horns tapped the glass in an irregular rhythm.

150

Pete, who was a pharmacist and the only one who knew of Matt's scheme, had set Matt up with the equipment and instructions to turn the slime of horned fish into white powder that he could sell. The kitchen table was stuffed with equipment, and the counters had bottles and other apparatus lined up along the edge. It hadn't been easy to learn, but Pete was patient and Matt persistent, and together they had figured it out. Pete wanted his cut, of course, but Matt was okay with that. He wouldn't have been able to do any of this without his cousin's guidance.

Matt walked the cooler over to the row of tanks then hesitated. It had been a long trip and he wanted nothing more than to crack open a beer on the lawn chair in front, but he should extract some product from his new fish. He didn't want to waste a batch, and since this fish was freshly caught, it would be dripping with the stuff. Once it sloughed off the slime onto the tank bottom, the stuff was a bitch to extract from feces and who knew what else was down there. Matt harvested slime from the fish three times a day when he could manage it, which was enough time for them to produce a thick coating of the stuff, but not long enough for it to drip off.

He slung the cooler onto a chair and found a pair of gloves that looked reasonably clean. He was careful not to touch the outside of the gloves, in case there was any leftover slime on them. He'd tested the product on himself, of course—it was a show-stopper—but he had things to do and didn't want to waste time on crazy visions.

He found a clean metal baking sheet—bought from a thrift store near his house—and opened the cooler. With sure movements, he jabbed his fingers into the fish's gills and yanked it up. The fish squirmed and writhed, but it couldn't escape. Matt pressed it against the baking sheet where it flopped with clanking and booming against the metal. The other fish tapped against their glass tanks in an agitated way, but Matt ignored them. They always got jumpy at harvesting time.

Smoothly, but without unnecessary gentleness, Matt scraped a butter knife from the gills to the tail. Viscous globs of slime pooled on the baking sheet. The fish squirmed harder. Matt flipped it over and repeated the motion on the other side, then carried the flopping fish over to the tanks and dropped it into an empty one.

"You're next," he said to the other fish. "But I need a beer first, so you'll have to wait."

Matt's back pocket vibrated. He stripped off his gloves, dropped them on the table, and slid his phone out.

"Hey, baby," he said.

"Hi, big boy," his girlfriend Bianca purred. "I miss you. What are you doing?"

Matt had told her he was on a job for a few weeks. It kept her from asking too many questions and gave him time to work on his plan. He wasn't sure what he would do after that, but he would think of something.

"Just work. I'd rather be home with you."

He looked at the baking sheet of slime. It could wait. He opened the fridge and balanced the sheet on top of a stack of containers. While he was there, he grabbed a beer. Bianca sighed on the other end of the line.

"It's such a waste. I bought a cute new bra, and I have no one to show."

"Hold on, baby. I'll be home soon." He would have loved to continue this conversation, but since he was pretending to be at work, it would reveal his lies. He changed the topic to distract himself from the memory of Bianca's curves, legendary among the men of Sayward. He still wasn't sure how he had managed to keep Bianca as his girlfriend, but he wasn't about to let her go anytime soon. "Any news from home?"

"Oh, yes. Stacy texted me. Her boyfriend took her to

Vegas, a surprise trip. She had no idea it was coming. Isn't that romantic? What a sweet guy."

"A surprise trip to Vegas?" Matt said slowly. He'd never considered such a thing. How much did flights and hotel cost? Not to mention food and shopping. Bianca loved shopping, when she could get it. "Do you like that kind of thing?"

"Oh, Matty," Bianca said in an indulgent tone. "What girl doesn't?"

Matt nodded to himself. Once sales of Sea Salt took off, he wouldn't be asking how much a trip to Vegas would cost. He would simply go and book it. Maybe he could propose to Bianca in Vegas. Yes, that would be perfect.

"Don't worry, baby," he said. "I have a good feeling about the future. There are lots of surprises coming our way."

ZEBALLOS

Corrie had retreated to the lab, and Krista had the boat underway for the next station. Jules followed Zeb into the galley.

"So?" Jules said. "What happened?"

"I messed up his propeller pretty bad." Zeb dug into a cupboard, searching for his dried jellyfish.

"Get out of my galley," Jules said indignantly. "You're screwing with my system."

"There's a good reason." Zeb's fingers closed on the package, and he pulled it out in triumph and held it up to Jules. "Want to go fishing?"

It took Jules a moment before understanding crossed his face, and then excitement.

"You saw the bait?" He realized what Zeb was holding up. "You're kidding, right? No one but you likes that stuff."

"Apparently, both strolias and Larry would disagree." Zeb tossed the package to Jules, who caught it with an incredulous look. "Set up the line while we're diving. See if anything bites."

"Aye, aye, captain." Jules examined the package with a shake of his head. "I hope you're right about this. I don't want to touch the stuff more than I have to. It gives me the heebie jeebies, remembering that rubber feeling in my mouth."

When Krista announced through the intercom that they were at the next station, Zeb went to the aft deck to get ready for diving. Jules already had his rod in the rod holder, his line in the water, and was whistling tunelessly. Zeb grabbed a bucket, filled it with water from the seawater hose on deck, and quietly placed it beside Jules.

"You're hopeful," Jules said.

"Better to be prepared than not."

Corrie came out with her fleece gear on, ready to put on her dry suit. When she spotted Jules, she looked confused.

"Fishing? Is that safe while we're diving?"

"We'll follow the shelf that way," Zeb said quickly, pointing to the far side of the boat. "We won't meet the hook underwater, I promise."

"And think how happy you'll be at dinner, when you bite into succulent, fresh fish." Jules smacked his lips. "Ever had it this fresh? There's nothing quite like it."

"Okay," said Corrie with a doubtful expression. "If you're sure."

Their dive was successful, although Zeb's itching skin screamed to be released from the confines of the wetsuit. When they surfaced, he could hardly wait another moment.

"You go on up," he told Corrie. "I want to check something on the bow. Bit of a mark there, make sure it's okay."

"Oh, right." She looked worried. "Do you want me to come and help?"

"I won't be long." Having her accompany him to the phantom mark would definitely not help. "I won't be diving, just swimming. Maybe I could pass my tank and weights up to you."

"Sure thing."

Once Corrie was out of sight and the sounds of the winch for water collection had started, Zeb wriggled out of his wetsuit with a gasp of relief. He tied the arms around the lowest rung of the ladder so that the suit wouldn't float away, then he flipped his body headfirst. His legs waved in the air until they reached the resistance of water, then he was diving. Sweet, glorious water flowed over him.

He stayed submerged for only a few minutes. Every ten seconds, he felt the almost indiscernible pulse from the strange device near the bow. He should search the wheelhouse when he was back on board. It was disconcerting to have unknown devices on his boat. On the surface, he untied his wetsuit and climbed quietly up the ladder. Corrie leaned over the railing to watch her bottles ascend, so he tiptoed to find his towel. A shout from Jules made him whirl around.

"Something's on the line!"

Zeb leaped to the rod, which was bent in a semicircle toward the water. He wrestled the rod from its holder and let the reel spin. It had worked for Matt, after all, and Zeb had plenty of experience winding in salmon. When the line grew slack, he reeled it in.

"Keep it taut," Jules said. "Nice steady pressure."

"This is not my first rodeo," Zeb said with gritted teeth. Corrie leaned over the railing beside him.

"What do you think you caught?" she said with interest. "Is it a salmon? Ling cod? Rockfish? Some rockfish are endangered, you know."

"We'll throw it back if we need to," Jules assured her. Zeb concentrated on his rod. The line tugged violently, and he let the reel spin once more.

"How many times do you do that?" Corrie asked.

"Until the fish is too tired to run," Jules said. "It's a game of endurance, for sure. We'll get it, though. Zeb's patience and my superb coaching will bag this fish."

Zeb grunted and reeled in the now-slack line.

"You're indispensable, you are."

"I know." Jules picked up a net from a hook nearby. "Hurry up, will you? We need to finish collecting water."

"Why don't I take the net, and you can pull the bottles up, Jules?" Corrie said. "I'd like my water on board as quickly as possible after our dive."

Jules handed her the net and moved to the winch. Zeb let the fish run one more time, but it was tiring, for it had hardly started running when it stopped again. Zeb wound in the slack, ready to pull this mystery fish out of the water. Was it a strolia? Could they be that lucky?

"Aren't you cold?" Corrie said. "You're only wearing a speedo, and the wind is freezing."

"I'm fine," Zeb said in distraction. There wasn't much resistance on the line anymore. "I don't mind the cold."

A silvery shape emerged from the gloom. Corrie squinted beside him.

"Wait," Corrie said. "What kind of fish is that?"

Zeb's heart gave a jolt of excitement. *Please, please, please,* he thought. *Let it be a strolia. Let me get it on board.*

"Ready with that net?" he said to Corrie. "I'm bringing it up now."

She held the net out in readiness, her brow furrowed with uncertainty. Zeb reeled the fish to the surface, then with a sudden motion, yanked it out of the water.

The strolia wriggled furiously in the open air, its scales glinting colorfully in the sun. Corrie gasped.

"The net!" Zeb shouted. "Hold it under!"

Corrie thrust the net out and Zeb lowered the squirming fish into it. Immediately, a growing hole formed in the rope where the horn sliced it open. Zeb swore and dropped the rod to grab the net from Corrie. He brought it to the deck and gingerly upended the fish into the bucket of saltwater. With a careful twist of his fingers, Zeb pulled out the hook from the fish's lip.

The fish stopped flailing but swam in endless circles in its circular prison. Zeb wiped sweat off his forehead. It might be cold out, but exertion and exhilaration had heated him.

"Is that—" Corrie said quietly. "Is that a unicorn fish?" She raised shining eyes to Zeb's. His face cracked open in a wide smile.

"Yeah. Yeah, it is."

KRISTA

Jules swung into the cabin, his breath coming in gasps. Krista looked at him askance.

"Maybe you should exercise more, Jules, if using the winch winded you that much."

"Krista!" he ignored her jibe. "We caught one. A unicorn fish!"

Krista stared at Jules, her brain trying to decipher his announcement. Somehow, after days of failure, they had managed to bring one of Zeb's infamous strolias on board. A part of her was distressed that Zeb's obsession was being fed, although maybe finding out that it was just a fish would help dispel any illusions about hidden worlds that he had. Another part of her was intensely curious to see the fish up close.

"Go on, go check it out," Jules said. "I'll take the wheel."

Krista shrugged, more for Jules' benefit than because she was indifferent, and headed to the aft deck. Zeb and Corrie kneeled beside a bucket that was usually used for cleaning the boat. Krista forced herself to walk slowly over.

"What did you find?" she asked. Zeb couldn't tear his eyes away from the bucket, but Corrie looked up with wide eyes.

"We got a unicorn fish." She shuffled over to make room. "Come see. It's amazing."

Even Krista had to admit that the unicorn fish, Zeb's strolia, was beautiful. For a fish. Its scales glistened with an iridescence she had never seen before, and the horn that sprouted above its eyes was composed of delicate, translucent bones. It swam around and around its tiny enclosure, and Krista's heart squeezed unexpectedly.

"Zeb, come on," she said sharply. "Get the poor thing a tank. It can hardly move in there."

Zeb leaped to his feet and lifted the cover of the hold. He

returned shortly with the aquarium tank, shoving it up and sliding it along the deck to a shaded spot behind the winch. Corrie jumped to fetch the saltwater hose and fill the tank. Krista heaved the bucket into the air and shuffled over. The fish swam in its endless circle even faster with the sloshing of the water.

"Sorry, buddy," she said quietly. Then she dumped the contents of the bucket into the tank.

After a moment of panicked thrashing, the fish settled down and swam in slow circles, exploring its new home. Corrie, Zeb, and Krista knelt to stare at it again.

The fish was mesmerizing, and there wasn't much in this world that Krista felt qualified for such a descriptor. She could watch it for hours. It seemed happier now, or at least as comfortable as it could be in a small tank instead of in the ocean. Its eye watched the three of them as intently as they watched it.

Eventually, Zeb shifted.

"So, Corrie," he said hoarsely. Krista wondered what he was thinking right now. "Do you want to do any tests to it? Or document it somehow?"

"Yes." Corrie sat up with a start then scrambled to her feet. She looked around in distraction. "Yes, right. Document. Let me grab my stuff." She disappeared into the lab. Shuffling, banging noises drifted out the open door.

"Now what?" Krista said quietly to Zeb. "Now that you've caught one, where do you go from here?"

Zeb shook his head wordlessly, his eyes fixed on the unicorn fish.

"Let's see what Corrie finds out," he said finally. "Any information is more than what I have right now."

"What are you really looking for?" Krista said. It hadn't occurred to her until now, until they had a living creature in a tank on the deck, to ask what Zeb truly wanted to get out of finding the basis of his mother's stories. Some convoluted path to figure out why he could hold his breath for so long? Some minor way to feel closer to his dead mother? Krista suspected Zeb didn't have a good answer.

He was spared from making something up by the return of Corrie. Her hands were full of sampling apparatus.

"Okay," Corrie said breathlessly. "I brought a camera, obviously, as well as swabs. I don't want to do anything more invasive at this point. Let's do preliminary testing first."

Krista's mouth twisted. She didn't want to see the unicorn fish—she refused to call it a strolia, even in her mind—hurt. It couldn't help being so strange.

"What will the swabs do?" she asked. Corrie prepared a plastic sampling bag.

"We can get a chemical composition of any exudates on its skin. See how it looks a bit slimy? I want to know what compounds are in it, especially if the slime is what causes hallucinations. I'll swab the skin, and then the blood on its mouth, if I can manage it. Blood would be far more likely to give me a clear genetic signal, and we can get information on exactly what sort of fish we are looking at."

Krista nodded, impressed despite herself. Maybe having Corrie along would prove useful, after all. If anything, they could find out that this fish was just a mutant salmon, and Zeb could get back to his regular life.

The skin swab was easy enough to get. Corrie sealed a bag around the swab then approached the fish for a second time. It flung itself around the tank in a skittish fashion. Krista gritted her teeth.

"You're scaring it," she snapped. "Wait a minute."

Corrie pulled the swab out with a surprised look on her face, but Krista ignored her and wriggled onto her stomach so that her head was level with the tank. She stared at the fish, trying to think. It swam around in an agitated circle, but when she traced her finger gently along the side of the tank, it followed her finger with its nose.

"Zeb, can you calm it down—somehow?" Krista referred to his ability to charm any fish he met underwater. He'd even encountered some six-gill sharks from the depths, but they had done little more than nuzzle him and retreat. Zeb shook his head.

"Don't know what I could do from here."

Krista nodded. He wasn't in the water. Sounds probably traveled differently through the air, and the fish wouldn't even hear Zeb properly. She snapped her fingers as an idea occurred to her.

"What did you use for bait? Put a bit of that on the swab, then get your sample while it's eating."

"Yes," Corrie breathed. "What did you use, after all?"

Zeb retrieved the package of dried jellyfish and fished out a piece. Corrie frowned.

"Jellyfish? Really? Okay, give it to me and I'll thread it onto the swab. I don't want you to touch the end of the swab without gloves."

The jellyfish threaded, Corrie plunged the swab into the tank. The fish skittered away at the sudden movement.

"Here," Krista said. "Let me try."

Corrie wavered, then she shrugged and handed Krista a pair of gloves. Once Krista had pulled on the thin latex over her hands, Corrie handed her the swab.

"One quick swipe will do. I can work with very little DNA, if necessary."

Krista nodded and slid the swab and jellyfish into the water. She waved it slowly. The fish looked at it intently. Then, slowly, so slowly, it swam toward the treat. Krista held her breath. Would this work?

The fish reached out and nibbled cautiously at the jellyfish. She pushed the swab closer to the wound on its lip. Closer, and closer, until...

"Yes," Corrie whispered. "You can bring it out anytime, now."

161

Krista let the fish finish its snack, then she carefully removed the swab from the water. Corrie waited with a sampling bag, and she sealed the swab inside.

Jules' voice crackled over the intercom.

"Will somebody please give me an update? I'm dying with curiosity up here."

CORRIE

Zeb went to the wheelhouse to tell Jules what had happened. Corrie left Krista to watch over the fish while she entered the lab. Although she wanted to do nothing else except stay next to the unicorn fish, she had water to filter. It had already waited too long.

After she had set up the filter equipment, and the water was dripping into her flask, Corrie opened her computer to check email. There was a message waiting for her from her supervisor, and her heart sank. What did he want this time? Two emails in as many days had to be a record for him.

Hello Corrie, please update more frequently while you are on the boat. Daily would be best. Have you analyzed any more data? Jonathan

Corrie groaned. Daily reports? Her sampling schedule was grueling, and that wasn't including their search for the unicorn fish. She barely had time to sleep as it was, and he wanted data?

Corrie poured more water into her filter apparatus, and, grumbling, pulled up the raw data from her most recent analysis. It meant very little without other data which she wouldn't be able to analyze until she was back in the lab, but it would do. Her supervisor would have to be satisfied with that, because she didn't have anything else.

Her fingers paused on the keyboard. She did have news, huge news. They had a unicorn fish in a tank, and she was sampling it. That would satisfy all of Jonathan's inquiries and doubts. A part of her balked at telling him. That part was much larger than the part that wanted to look competent in her supervisor's eyes. The unicorn fish was her discovery, hers and the crew's. It was her interest in legendary creatures that had fueled the search, not her other project. It still felt too close to the contents of her blog. Even with hard evidence swimming in a tank on the deck, she was still nervous about her secret obsession being exposed. Also, she wanted to find a few answers before Jonathan swooped in on her discovery. Maybe it was a petty reason—she should care more about furthering scientific knowledge than about her own stake in it—but she couldn't shake the feeling. What Jonathan didn't know wouldn't hurt him.

She cobbled together a figure and sent it off with promises of daily reports. Her eyes fell on the swabs. Answers were lying on the counter, waiting to be found. Corrie poured more water into her filter, snapped on a new pair of gloves with gusto, and started to prepare samples from the swabs. If she was quick, she might be done by late afternoon.

During a break in her analysis, she emailed a friend in the sequencing lab at the university, who routinely analyzed samples for their genetic makeup.

Hi Robert, I have a really big ask. Could you amplify a few samples for me using generic primers for fish, then run them on your next sequencing run? I can have the samples arrive by tomorrow. I know this is so big, but I will pay you in cash, fine dining, work-in-lieu, the moon, or whatever you consider fair payment. Please? Corrie

Zeb popped his head into the lab as she pressed send.

"Lunch soon."

"Change of plans," Corrie said. "Where's the nearest town with a post office?"

ZEBALLOS

Bringing Corrie along on this trip had been a huge gamble, but it was paying massive dividends. Zeb hadn't expected to meet anyone as interested in the secrets of the sea as him, but he was constantly surprised by Corrie. She had a stubborn determination and an insane work ethic in pursuit of the answers of the strolia. She had still been in the lab last night when he had gone to bed, and now she had worked through lunch today to have her samples ready to mail.

Zeb glanced at her face as she gazed out over the rolling sea and felt a wave of admiration for Corrie. She, Zeb, and Krista were on their way to Lund to mail Corrie's samples and buy more bait. Corrie said that they might have a response for the genetic work in a few days, if they were very lucky. Zeb hoped so. He didn't know what the samples would tell them, but any information was good information.

Corrie caught his eye.

"What about a catch-and-release program?" she said, excitement coloring her voice. "Then we could find out population numbers, migration patterns—now that we know what bait they are attracted to, it would be straightforward."

"Could we follow them?" Zeb asked. Krista glanced at him searchingly. Corrie shrugged in uncertainty.

"I think so, but radio tags are pretty expensive, and I don't know how small they make them. They're usually used for whales. But maybe." Corrie jiggled her leg while she thought. "Regular tags, though, I could probably rustle up at the university. Then later in the summer I could come back and tag them, or I could teach you how to do it. It's easy enough, especially if you have experience catching fish."

"I have that." Zeb glanced at Krista, whose face was stormy. When would she get it through her brain that he was doing this, whether she liked it or not? He looked pointedly away and focused instead on Corrie's declaration that she would come back on the boat later in the summer. He found himself looking forward to it. This trip so far was intense, thrilling, and the four of them made a good team. When Krista wasn't glowering at everyone, that is.

At the dock, Zeb pointed in the direction of the post office and Corrie raced away. Zeb and Krista followed her more sedately, their target a grocery store three blocks away.

"What do you like about dried jellyfish?" Krista asked, out of the blue. Zeb thought for a moment.

"I don't know. Why does anyone like anything? It's salty, chewy, and I crave it sometimes. Why do you like chocolate-covered raisins so much?"

Krista didn't answer him directly.

"I wonder why Larry the fisherman was eating it. He doesn't seem like the type to experiment with flavors."

"I bet his brother's wife got him into it. Jules said she's Chinese. I don't know how he knew that—he gets people talking, I guess."

"Maybe your mum was part Chinese. She introduced you to dried jellyfish, right?"

"I don't know what she was," Zeb said with finality. That was the whole reason for this escapade, to find out more about her and, by extension, about Zeb. He didn't have much to go on, except that his mother's life before he was born was foggy with mystery, she was different like him, and she told fantastical stories. That was the sum of his knowledge. Chinese? Maybe, but Zeb was pretty sure there was more to the story than an Asian heritage.

Krista brought up a good point, though. When he wanted jellyfish, he really craved it. Jellyfish never seemed to quench the craving, but the desire faded on its own eventually. Did the strolias feel the same? If so, why?

JULES

The *Clicker* was anchored in Lund's harbor, and Jules was in the galley, preparing dinner. Chicken cordon bleu tonight, and he sliced a side of carrots into slender sticks for quicker cooking. His phone played music loudly, and he belted out the lyrics right along with it. It was strange being on his own on the boat—the solitude reminded him uncomfortably of hours on his own after school as a child—but it was strangely pleasant, for the same reason. Days on the *Clicker*, constantly in each other's faces, grated after a while. He'd be glad to see the others come back, but, for now, he was enjoying blasting his music without Krista stomping in and turning it off.

Something large and heavy clanked against the metal hull of the *Clicker*. Jules frowned and turned off his music. Were the others back already? It felt like they'd only just left. He'd hardly done any kitchen prep yet. Jules wiped his hands on a tea towel and wandered outside.

He stopped abruptly. The man outside wasn't Zeb, not even close. His ash blond hair was the only similarity between them. This man was at least a head taller than Jules, and muscly where he was wiry. His severe face completed the don't-mess-with-me look. Jules would have liked to comply, but this was the *Clicker*. Only friends of Zeb were allowed on, and Jules knew that this man was no friend.

"Matt Nielsen," he said clearly, keeping the waver out of his voice that threatened to emerge. "What the hell do you think you're doing here?"

"Getting a message across," Matt said in a deep, rough voice. "You tampered with my boat yesterday. Don't know how, but I'm sure it was your lot. Had to call the coast guard to tow me home." He took a step closer to Jules, who stood his ground even though every cell in his body screamed at him to retreat. "I don't like threats, and I don't like anyone messing with my boat. Or fucking around in my business."

"Got it," said Jules. "No fucking. Now, get off the boat."

"When I'm ready." Matt looked around. "You're too interested in my business. It got me thinking, why? Do you have a stake in it? I'm not interested in competition."

He took a step toward the aft deck, and Jules thought in horror of the unicorn fish in its tank. It was covered by some shade cloth, but that wouldn't stop someone truly searching.

"I don't know what you're talking about," Jules said, his voice raised. "But get off the *Clicker*, right now. You don't like competition? I don't like trespassers." Jules glanced around for a weapon, anything he could use to hold his ground against the larger man. A gaff hook rested on a rack against the hull, and he grabbed it and held it up. Matt looked at him and laughed. It was a chilling sound.

"You think you can gaff me like a fish?" He took a fire ax off the wall of the cabin and planted his feet squarely. "I'd like to see you try. Go on, give me a laugh."

The roar of an approaching engine entered Jules' ears, but didn't penetrate his brain. His eyes scanned Matt's body, looking for ideas of where to strike with his hook. He knew this was a fool's errand, that Matt would likely grab the hook out of his hands and toss it away, but he had to try.

Matt took a step closer, and Jules' knees wobbled like water. He gritted his teeth. Maybe he shouldn't bother. Let the big man take the fish and run. But the thought of Zeb's devastated face emboldened Jules.

"Get off the boat," he yelled. "I won't ask again."

The engine roared louder, and Matt turned to look. Quicker than his doubtful thoughts, Jules darted the pole toward him and hooked the end around the other man's thigh. It stuck, and Matt let out a yell of anguish. He turned to Jules with murder in his eyes.

"What the fuck do you think you're doing, Matt?" Krista's voice screamed from the dinghy. She had lungs on her, that

168

one. "Get the hell away from Jules!"

Matt ripped the hook out of his thigh with a grunt of pain. He smashed the hook to the ground and held the ax over his head. Jules backed away.

With a clang, the dinghy bumped into the *Clicker*. Moments later, Zeb climbed on board with Krista right behind him. Matt turned at the sound.

"Get off my boat," Zeb said with eerie calm. In contrast, Krista quivered with fiery rage.

"You heard him," she shouted. "Off."

Matt must have realized that he was outnumbered, for he limped to the ladder. Zeb stepped aside to let him pass, but Krista stood for a moment in his path to glare before she moved. Matt climbed awkwardly down the ladder but paused to sneer at them.

"Stay out of my business. This is your last warning."

Nobody spoke until Matt had raced away. Jules leaned over the railing, the adrenaline rushing out of his body making his legs limp and his heart pound. Corrie was still in the dinghy, holding it steady against the *Clicker*.

"Are you okay?" she asked with a worried expression. Jules tried to smile, but it felt fake.

"Not a scratch. But I drew blood on the other guy. I win?"

"Let's get the dinghy up," Zeb said in a measured tone. Before he walked to the winch, his hand rested on Jules' shoulder. "I'm glad that idiot didn't hurt you."

"I'm glad you came back when you did," Jules answered.

After the dinghy was on board, Krista kicked the ax across the deck in frustration.

"That bastard. No one steps on the *Clicker* without permission. No one threatens our friends. No one!"

"I didn't know you cared," Jules said. Krista glared at him, but with less rancor than usual.

"This is getting serious," said Corrie in a small voice. "I don't want anyone to get hurt because I'm studying the

169

unicorn fish."

"It wasn't only your decision," said Zeb.

"Do we stop now?" said Corrie. "It looks like we're in the middle of a drug cartel."

"Cartel?" Krista snorted. "It's only that rat bastard catching unicorn fish and trying to make a profit. There is no 'cartel.' And, I don't know about you, but I want to bring him down. We have to stop him. Not only is he exploiting an unregulated species and producing illicit drugs, he's resorting to brute force and threats to get his way. I won't stand for it."

"I understand if you want to stop," Zeb said to Corrie, although Jules could tell that he didn't mean it. Zeb wanted to hunt unicorn fish, and Corrie was his best tool to do that. "We can finish your week on the boat, drop you off in Vancouver, and I can bring Matt to justice."

"No, I—" Corrie gulped. "I want to know more about it. I'm willing to take the risk. I just don't want you all to feel obligated to put yourselves in danger for my projects."

"I'm for it, and Krista has made her view clear," said Zeb. He turned to Jules with a pleading look in his eyes. "Jules, what do you want to do?"

Jules hesitated. Matt's severe face floated in his mind's eye, and the fear it evoked flushed through his system once again. He truly hadn't known the outcome of that scenario, if the others hadn't arrived when they did. His trailer in Campbell River wasn't far. He could be back on dry land in a matter of hours.

But this was Zeb's dream. Zeb was a friend who didn't ask for much, and he was always there for Jules. Jules asked Zeb for plenty. Cash, jobs, someone to entertain him, a wingman. Could he desert his best friend?

Man up, he told himself sternly. *Do it for Zeb.*

"I'm in," he said in a hearty tone. "Someone needs to feed you bunch. You'd probably resort to beans on toast every night if I weren't here to save you."

Zeb's shoulders loosened in relief, and Jules knew he'd made the right choice. Now, if only his heart would stop palpitating and get with the program.

"How do we get the slimy bastard?" Krista said. "Fishing without a permit?"

"That's so hard to patrol," Zeb said. "They likely wouldn't investigate unless they actually saw him pull in a fish."

"More boat sabotage?" Jules suggested. At Zeb's wide eyes and Corrie's questioning glance, he backtracked. "You know, his motor broke the other day, somehow—could we make that happen again? Hard to fish without a boat."

"Don't know how we'd do that without him noticing," Krista said with a quelling look at Jules. "What about getting him for assault?"

"His word against ours, and he's the one with the hole in his leg," Zeb said. "It doesn't look good. Let's hope he doesn't take his side of the story to the authorities."

"What if we go to his home and release the unicorn fish he already has?" said Corrie. "That would be a start."

"I could probably find out where he lives," said Krista. "It's not a bad idea. But, just a warning, his family is into hunting. He might be licensed for firearms. Plus, he's massive. Any attack on his home would have to be done with loads of stealth."

Corrie and Zeb looked downcast, and Krista grim.

"Let's think about it over dinner," Jules said. He didn't have any answers, but at least he had food to offer. "It'll be ready in half an hour."

CORRIE

Corrie didn't sleep well that night. Visions of Jules facing off against Matt Nielsen kept visiting her mind, growing more horrible every time. By the end, a flock of flying unicorn fish were swooping down on the two above a boat made of carrots that was sinking into filtered seawater.

No one spoke much at breakfast, except to confirm the location of their next station. There must have been no brainwaves in the night. Corrie thought that rescuing unicorn fish from Matt's house was the simplest idea. Krista must have felt the same, because she disappeared into their cabin to phone old acquaintances for Matt's home address.

Corrie and Zeb dived for samples, and she and Jules collected water, but her heart wasn't in it. She filtered water in the lab with only half an eye on it. The rest of her time was spent analyzing samples and staring at the unicorn fish in its tank. It stared balefully back at her and tapped the glass with its horn as it swam in circles.

Now that she had a legendary creature in her keeping, she wasn't sure what to do with it. She'd already photographed it, taken plenty of notes about it, sent samples for sequencing— what else did one do with a new species? Maybe she could do some behavioral studies, see how it reacted to different stimuli. Corrie gathered a few supplies and went to the aft deck.

Krista was already there, kneeling beside the tank and staring into it with a soft expression that Corrie hadn't known she was capable of. It hardened into its usual sternness when Krista noticed Corrie.

"I'm going to run some tests," Corrie said by way of explanation, although she didn't know why she needed to explain herself. Krista's eyes narrowed.

"Is that necessary?"

"Absolutely," Corrie said, irritated by Krista. Why was she here, questioning Corrie's expertise? Corrie may not know how to drive a boat, but science was her thing. Then she caught Krista's worried glance at the tank and understood. "It's not going to hurt the fish, I promise. Spiky might even find it fun."

"Spiky?"

"Unicorn fish is kind of cumbersome to say all the time," Corrie kneeled and arranged some objects on the deck floor. "It needed a name. Do you have a better one?"

"Any name would be better than Spiky," Krista muttered. She looked at the fish, and it tapped the glass with its horn. "But sure. Spiky works."

Corrie carefully placed a small cutting board in one end of the tank to divide part of it in half.

"What's the idea?"

"It's called conditioned place preference." Corrie pulled out her notebook. "It's a test for memory and cognition. We'll put a piece of jellyfish in one side as a positive stimulus, and I'll tap the glass if it goes to the other side as a negative stimulus. Then, we'll see if it prefers one side over the other. See if it can differentiate between them. We know absolutely nothing about this creature, so any information we can get is interesting. I need to take a few more notes on its physical features, as well. Did you check out the ventral side, its underside? It's slightly flattened and almost cupped. I wonder what it's for."

They spent the next half hour doing all the tests that Corrie could recall from her animal behavior class in undergrad. By the end, Krista was smiling and talking to Spiky. Corrie pretended not to notice, but inside she was flabbergasted at Krista's display of a softer side. She left the last test and her notebook for Krista to complete and went into the lab to finish an analysis.

Her phone indicated she had an email. It was from Robert,

her friend in the sequencing lab. Corrie almost dropped the phone in her haste to check it.

Hi Corrie, I got the samples this morning, and lucky you, I had time to amplify and run a gel. The fish primers I used didn't work, but I have a few more to try. I'll keep you posted. Robert

Corrie turned off the screen and stared out her tiny window at an island beyond. Robert must have made a mistake. Maybe his chemicals were old. The fish primers should have worked. What else was the unicorn fish, if not a fish?

Unless they really were dealing with a legendary creature. Corrie jiggled her leg in thought. This was why she hadn't told her supervisor yet. She needed to know more about what they were dealing with before he found out. Corrie's interest was well and truly piqued, and she didn't want her cryptozoology and biology sides to intersect quite yet. How could she explain the fish? Where would it fit on an evolutionary tree, if she couldn't even get the DNA sequenced? It had to fit. Nothing on this earth couldn't be slotted into place, ordered and accounted for. She needed more evidence, more answers, more proof, before she brought the unicorn fish to her supervisor's attention. She needed more answers for herself.

KRISTA

Krista wrote the last finding in Corrie's notebook and snapped it shut. The unicorn fish twitched.

"Sorry, Spiky," she said softly. "I didn't mean to scare you."

She reached into her pocket and withdrew a piece of jellyfish. She held it over the top of the tank and dropped it gently into the water. The fish's horn crested the surface as it snatched the jellyfish with its mouth and swallowed it whole. Krista smiled.

"Have a good snack, Spiky." She stood and dusted off her jeans. "I'll be back soon, I promise."

Krista dropped off the notebook with Corrie, who was frowning at her phone, then wandered through the galley. She snuck a piece of cheese from a cutting board while Jules was at the stove then raised her eyebrow when he huffed at her. She took an exaggerated bite and chewed slowly while staring at him. Jules waved her away with a knife.

"Get out of the kitchen, woman. This is my domain."

"Refreshing words," she said. "But my family is paying for this cheese, so I'll eat it whenever I want."

She turned toward the wheelhouse and smiled at the exaggerated sigh from behind her. Jules might be an idiot, but he wasn't half-bad company. She couldn't handle him for long, of course, but a week on the boat was manageable. Having Jules on board kept Zeb happy, or at least more grounded.

Zeb was at the wheel, driving to their next station. His hair was still damp from his latest post-diving swim. Krista tried to ignore it. She perched on the foldout seat.

"Corrie might know what she's talking about, sometimes," she said with another bite of her cheese. Zeb gave her an incredulous look.

175

"High praise, coming from you. Why, how did she impress you?"

"We ran some tests, looking at how the fish reacted to different things. We collected some interesting information. I don't know what it all means yet, but still."

"Helping with the science, now?"

"Yeah, well, I wanted to make sure she didn't hurt Spiky."

Krista pressed her lips together after the fish's name passed her lips. Damn. Zeb wouldn't let that one pass. True to form, Zeb let out a snort.

"Spiky? You named it?"

"Corrie did," she defended herself.

"You used it."

"Shut up." It was ridiculous, her care for the fish. The way it looked at her, though, with hopeful eyes and a tilt to its head, like it wanted to tell her something... She shook her head in disgust at herself. It was a fish. She ate them for dinner. Not the ones with horns, but still. She changed the topic to one that would wipe all mirth from Zeb's face.

"What are we going to do about Matt?" she said. Zeb frowned.

"I honestly don't know."

"I do," she said. Zeb looked at her and she elaborated. "You drop me off on his boat, I beat him up, you get the fish. Done deal."

Zeb shook his head with a small smile.

"Have you seen the size of him? I know you're scrappy, but I'm pretty sure he's not going to act the gentleman with you."

"Okay, we follow him down a dark alley, you, me, and Jules jump him, tie him up, and leave him on the police station doorstep with something illegal in his pocket."

"Like what?"

"I don't know, I'm brainstorming here. Honestly, Zeb, try to keep up. Contribute a little."

"I'd like to avoid any scenario that involves us attempting to beat up the modern-day Viking," Zeb said. His smile faded. "But I don't know what to do about him."

There was a rustle at the doorway, and Corrie entered. Zeb stiffened, and his body oriented itself in Corrie's direction. Krista narrowed her eyes.

"Trying to figure out what to do about Matt?" Corrie said. "I'm out of ideas, too."

"Dead end after dead end," Krista said flatly. "We'll have to decide soon, though, or else your time on the boat will be up."

Corrie sighed.

"Keep thinking, I guess. Hey, could one of you give me a hand? I want to change the water in Spiky's tank. It's getting a bit murky."

"I can," Zeb said quickly. "Krista, could you take the wheel?"

Krista nodded, and Zeb followed Corrie out the door. Krista frowned. Zeb was acting strangely around Corrie, and she didn't like it. Anything out of the ordinary with Zeb was perilous. He was extraordinary enough.

CORRIE

"I think Spiky is excreting something," Corrie said over her shoulder as Zeb followed her through the lab to the aft deck. "There's a bunch of slime on the bottom and sides."

"Don't touch it," Zeb said quickly. "It's probably what causes the hallucinations."

"No worries there." Corrie pulled out two sets of latex gloves from her pocket and handed Zeb a pair. "I brought protection." She smiled playfully at Zeb, who looked down in confusion. Was he shy? Maybe innuendos weren't advisable with Zeb, at most her colleague, at least her sponsor. Living with these three people on a small boat for five days made Corrie forget how little they knew each other. She cleared her throat.

"Let's transfer the fish into a bucket. I'll scrub the tank and we'll pour the water overboard then fill it up again with the saltwater hose. It should be quick, and the fish will have a nice clean home again."

Zeb nodded and fetched a bucket.

"Can I slide it right into the tank?" he asked.

"Yep. Less traumatic than a net."

Zeb dipped the bucket into the fish's tank. Though it squirmed away from the bucket, Zeb managed to trap it in a corner and scoop it up. Corrie grabbed a sponge she had tied to the other end of a short net.

"Give me a minute to scrub away the worst of this slime."

The slime was translucent and colorless, and slid off the sides of the glass tank easily. It clung with a vengeance to the sponge, however, and it took Corrie a half-minute of swishing and banging to dislodge the worst of it from her cleaning tool. Zeb disappeared while she was cleaning and reappeared with a different hose.

"There's no way we're picking the tank up," he said.

"And I don't want that slime on my deck, especially if it's toxic. We'll siphon the water out and dump it directly into the ocean."

"How are you going to start the suction?" she asked.

"Very carefully," he said. Before Corrie could ask what he meant, Zeb stuck a hose end in the tank and lay down on the deck. He put his mouth to the other end and sucked air through the hose.

"Zeb!" Corrie said, scandalized. "What if you get a whole mouthful of toxic seawater in your mouth?" He clearly hadn't taken the safety courses that she had. He shrugged and sucked again then shoved the end of the hose through a drainage hole in the bulwark. Water gushed out and splashed into the sea beyond.

"See? It worked. No slime in my mouth, either."

Corrie shook her head. The tank emptied quickly, and while Zeb curled up the hose, Corrie filled the tank with clean water. She gently poured the fish back in, and it swam in circles to examine its clean home.

"There you go, Spiky," Corrie whispered. "Nice and clean."

Corrie looked up at the sound of a hose being dropped to the ground. Zeb hung over the side of the boat, his jaw slack.

"Holy shit," he breathed.

Corrie leaped to his side and followed his gaze. In the wake of their boat, a disturbance cut the waves in a boiling turbulence. Then, a tentacle appeared above the surface.

Corrie gripped the railing with white fingers. The only thing she could think at first was how enormous the tentacle was. It was at least twenty feet long, and that was only what emerged from the sea. It was a bruised-looking reddish purple, with almost translucent suckers from the tip of the tentacle to the base. It flailed and curled, and a hill of water mounded beside it as if something were about to surface. But nothing emerged, and the tentacle sank into the frothing

179

waves.

"What the hell was that?" Corrie squeaked. She could hardly push the words out. There was no air in her lungs. "That was so big! What could it have been? The biggest a Giant Pacific Octopus can get is usually a fifteen-foot arm span, and that was easily five times bigger. Maybe Architeuthis, a giant squid? Their tentacles can be forty-three feet long, which still isn't big enough, but that's the biggest cephalopod there is. But they don't come to the surface unless they're dead, and that was definitely not dead. No way. What else could it be?"

Corrie tried to stop her babbling, but in her shock, it was all she could think of to do. Zeb simply stared, mouth open, eyes scanning their wake for another sighting.

"I'm going to get my camera," Corrie blurted out. Documentation. That was key. In science as in life: pics or it didn't happen. She raced to the lab and grabbed her camera from its hook. She took a frenzied moment to thank her overly orderly self then leaped back outside.

"Did you see it again?" she gasped. Zeb shook his head.

"Should we turn back?" he said, more to himself than to Corrie.

Corrie's immediate thought was *hell, yes*. If this wasn't validation of her blog, then she didn't know what was. Then her logical brain took over. That tentacle was huge. How big was the creature underneath? Sailors' stories of sea monsters attacking ships floated through her mind, and she gulped. Was turning back really the smartest plan?

"I can't believe I'm saying this," Corrie said. "But maybe we shouldn't. How big was it, exactly? Could it be dangerous?"

"That's what I was wondering," Zeb replied, his eyes still scanning the ocean.

"But it's right there." Corrie jiggled her leg. How could they pass up this opportunity? But how could they put

180

themselves in so much danger? "But sea creatures can be unpredictable. Did you ever see that video of the whale breaching onto that huge sailboat?"

"Yeah." Zeb's normally stoic face twisted with indecision. "Yeah, we probably should keep moving."

"Why was it here?" Corrie asked. Her mind, stalled by shock, started to click forward once more. "Does it have a cave here? Is there something it's hunting for?"

Zeb finally tore his gaze away from the ocean at Corrie's question. He focused his pale eyes on her.

"Hunting," he said slowly. "What would it be hunting?" His eyes slid to the tank with Spiky inside, now covered with shade cloth. Corrie gasped.

"Do you think it was attracted to Spiky's slime?" Her heart thumped at the notion—it felt right—but she let her science brain take over. "It's a far-fetched theory, but one we can certainly test. Let's collect some more slime and throw it overboard."

"How much do we need?"

"As much as we can get. If the tentacle doesn't reappear, then either it isn't attracted to the slime, or we didn't put in enough and we'll have to try when we have more."

Corrie's hands trembled as she put on gloves and collected her sponge, still amply covered with slime despite her attempts to remove the gooey stuff. Zeb, in contrast, moved with swift, jerky motions, as if trying to suppress his eagerness. Corrie didn't know why he bothered. She would have jumped through the roof if they'd been under one. They were near a sea monster, a real-life sea monster, she was sure of it. Her heart pounded almost painfully in her chest. She was too young for an excitement-induced heart attack, right?

Corrie swished the sponge in the bucket of seawater that Zeb held out for her. She looked up at him.

"This is incredible," she whispered. "Can this really be happening? I've been searching for so many years. The

181

unicorn fish, this tentacle—these are legends coming to life. Are you my good luck charm?"

"I was going to ask you the same thing," Zeb said hoarsely. He cleared his throat. "Are you ready for round two?"

Corrie nodded.

"Let's do this."

ZEBALLOS

"Wait," Corrie said. She raced into the lab. Zeb gripped the bucket tightly. What was she doing? With every second, they were driving further and further away from the *brigar*. It couldn't be anything else. The suckers, that maroon skin—his mother hadn't told him many tales of the brigar, not enough to know whether it might be hunting strolias, but she had told him enough to recognize one when he saw it. He clenched the bucket and took large, steadying breaths, trying to compose himself before Corrie returned.

She did in a moment, holding out an eye dropper.

"No point in wasting slime if a tiny bit will do." She filled the eye dropper with water from the bucket. "Let's see how sensitive this beastie is."

Zeb was unconvinced, but he kept his mouth shut. What he wanted to do more than anything was to pour the entire contents of the bucket overboard and see the tentacle once more. He was tempted, almost beyond resistance, to dive in and look for the brigar with his own eyes, but he knew that was a terrible idea. Aside from revealing his strangeness to Corrie, his mother's stories had been clear: the brigar was not to be underestimated. It was huge, hungry, and could rarely be reasoned with.

Corrie leaned over the edge and emptied the eyedropper into the waves. Zeb wedged the bucket behind some rope and glued his eyes to the wake of the boat.

"How long until it can taste the slime?" he said, half to himself.

"Depends how sensitive it is," Corrie answered. "Sharks can smell blood from three miles away. If we don't see anything in," she checked her watch. "Two minutes, I'll pour a larger amount of slime water in."

"There!" Zeb stopped breathing again. The water behind

183

the boat bubbled and frothed in a pattern inconsistent with the lines of their wake. Corrie fumbled with her camera.

"Come on, come on," she breathed. "Show yourself, beastie."

As if it heard Corrie, a dark tentacle looped above the surface of the water. Zeb's heart stuttered. Corrie's camera clicked again and again. The tentacle slid back into the sea, and the surface waters closed behind it as if it had never been there. Corrie turned to Zeb with shining eyes.

"Can you believe it?" She threw herself at him and gave him a swift hug. Zeb barely had time to respond to her warm body pressed against his before she pushed away. "A unicorn fish and a sea monster? And they're clearly connected somehow. I don't know whether the tentacle thing is super hungry and really loves to eat unicorn fish, or maybe it's a different relationship, not predator-prey. Maybe they have a symbiosis of some kind. What could it be? How can we find out?" She checked herself and spoke in a slightly calmer voice. "Of course, there might not be a connection. We only tried putting the slime water overboard twice. The next time we do it, we might not be near a tentacle thing, and it won't be able to sense the slime. Unless there are lots of tentacle things everywhere..." Corrie gazed into the distance with awe.

"Your pictures," Zeb said urgently. "Can I see them? Zoom in?" Now that the brigar was gone again, he ached to see evidence of it. His mother's voice swirled in his head, snippets of stories echoing in his mind. First the strolias, now a brigar—what next? And how could he find his next creature? Krista would kill him for thinking of it, but now that he had seen two creatures from his mother's stories, it had only whetted his appetite. He needed to see more, know more. This was only the beginning.

Corrie turned the camera toward him, and they bent their heads together to see the tiny screen. Corrie flipped to a

184

picture that showed the largest amount of tentacle then zoomed in. Every sucker was in crisp detail, and even healed scars showed on the creature's arm.

"Wait," Zeb said. He pointed at the screen. "Zoom in on the base of the tentacle. We can almost see the body."

Corrie moved the image around. Sure enough, through the green water, dark body was visible. Zeb squinted.

"What's on the skin?"

They leaned closer. Corrie's hair tickled Zeb's ear.

"It looks like—" Corrie frowned. "Is that a horn?"

"There's a st—unicorn fish right beside it," Zeb said. "Why was it chasing our slime trail if it had a unicorn fish right there?"

"Unless the unicorn fish is attached to the tentacle thing," Corrie said with growing excitement. "Think about it. Why else would the unicorn fish have a strange flat spot on its ventral side? That's it. It's like a remora, sucked onto the side of the tentacle thing. Yes! They're symbiotic somehow. The tentacle thing isn't hunting unicorn fish. It's collecting them."

"What for?"

"That's another question." Corrie looked puzzled then brightened. "A question for the future. They must be important to the tentacle thing, though, because it's finely tuned to sense them in the water."

"But why didn't the tentacle thing collect the school of unicorn fish that we saw first?"

Corrie frowned in puzzlement.

"Maybe—maybe it's a signal that the unicorn fish gives out when it wants the protection of the tentacle thing." Excitement warmed her voice. "Yes! Maybe they only produce slime when they're scared, like getting caught in a net and being held captive in a tank. It's a working hypothesis, anyway."

That was something that Zeb hadn't been told. What other secrets were lurking in the ocean? Once again, he had to restrain himself from leaping overboard to find them.

KRISTA

Zeb marched into the wheelhouse, his face stormy, fearful, and hopeful all at once. Corrie was right behind him, wild-eyed, and Jules brought up the rear, looking confused. They all squeezed into the tiny wheelhouse. Krista shuffled sideways with pursed lips.

"What are you all doing here?" she said. "I don't remember inviting you to invade my space."

"I did," said Zeb. Shades of their father's gruff authority laced through his tone, and Krista grimaced. Apparently, there was an afterlife, if only through one's children. "Corrie and I just saw a—" Zeb took a deep breath. He was clearly struggling to compose himself, although Krista wondered if anyone but her would notice. "Something huge and tentacled in the water. Way bigger than any known octopus or squid."

"I'm calling it the tentacle thing for now," said Corrie. "But I'm open to suggestions."

Krista ignored her.

"What are you talking about?" she said in a quelling voice. That was all she needed, another creature for Zeb to obsess over. Maybe her mission was a futile one. How could she take care of her little brother, get him away from all this nonsense, if the odds were so stacked against her? And what the hell was with all these creatures, anyway? She growled internally at Clicker's memory. Why had she filled Zeb's head with mystery? Couldn't she have left him to be a regular kid?

"We can prove it," Zeb said stiffly. "Show them the pictures, Corrie."

Wordlessly, Corrie held out her camera with the screen pointing at Krista and Jules. Krista leaned in. An octopus arm rose from the waves. Her eyes widened when she compared the size of it to a nearby island in the photo. She frowned to cover her uncertainty and fear. What was it? Zeb gestured at the camera.

"The—tentacle thing." Zeb glanced at Corrie briefly, no doubt because he felt embarrassed at using the stupid name, as he should. "Is attracted to the slime of the unicorn fish. We dumped slime overboard, twice, and it surfaced both times."

"We didn't want you to stop the boat," Corrie said. "Because it was so massive that we were afraid it might attack the *Clicker*."

"You're saying that there's a giant sea monster under the boat right now?" Jules' normally pale face grew another shade of white. The lily-livered kid wouldn't take a stand against a snail.

"Yeah." Instead of looking worried, Corrie's face grew animated. "But think of it. Two new species! This is incredible. World-changing. But we have to do something about Matt. There is potentially a whole world of new sea creatures waiting to be discovered. What if they are endangered, and Matt is killing them all off? We could be seeing the last of their kind, and we wouldn't know. And the way he was treating that unicorn fish? It's animal cruelty. He has to be stopped."

"Yeah, okay," Krista said in a skeptical voice. "But what are we going to do about it?"

The wheelhouse was silent for a moment. Then Corrie's face lit up like a lighthouse.

"What if we use the tentacle thing to help us rescue unicorn fish? We can create a distraction for Matt, and then we sneak in and rescue the fish while he's busy."

Krista stared at the tiny, bubbly scientist. She hadn't expected a plan like that from Corrie. It sounded something Krista herself would come up with.

"It's foolhardy, ridiculous, and so full of holes I could stick a gaff hook through it," Krista said. "But it's a plan with style. I like it."

Corrie gave her a disbelieving smile then turned to Zeb. He nodded, his eyes thoughtful.

"It'll take some more planning, but I like it."

"It has the element of surprise, for sure," said Jules. His color had returned with Corrie's enthusiasm. "Couldn't Matt catch more, though? He only has to put some jellyfish on a hook, and he can refill his tanks with unicorn fish."

"We could destroy the equipment he uses to make the drug," Krista said with relish. "He's not rolling in money. He probably sunk a fair bit of coin into this venture. He won't recover easily if we trash his stuff."

"But where is Matt keeping the fish and all this equipment?" said Zeb. His face fell, and Krista's betraying heart twisted. Damn Zeb. He didn't make helping him easy. She gave a long-suffering sigh.

"I think I know where he is," she said. Zeb's eyes bored into her.

"Where?"

"His family has a cabin in Toba Inlet. The grandfather used it for fishing trips. I'll bet you anything that Matt's holed up there with his stolen unicorn fish."

"Toba Inlet," Zeb said slowly. "That's only a few hours away."

"Okay, okay, okay." Corrie was having a hard time getting her words out. Krista watched her with amusement. "So, I collect secretions to throw around to distract the tentacle thing."

"Like grenades," said Jules, who leaned forward in his interest. "I think I have something in the galley that we could make work."

"Yes!" Corrie turned shining eyes on Jules, then she frowned.

"I hope Matt doesn't hurt the tentacle thing."

"You said it could take down a boat?" Krista said. "I'd save your worry for Matt."

189

CORRIE

Corrie couldn't stop shaking from excitement and terror. They were on a rescue mission to save unicorn fish. They were going up against a dangerous criminal. They had just seen a tentacle thing.

Corrie's mind stuttered to a halt at that thought. A real, live, giant octopus of legendary proportions had emerged behind their boat. She wouldn't even know where to begin when she blogged this event. Where had the tentacle thing come from? How was it that they had spotted two legendary creatures in less than a week? And how was this creature related to other octopuses? How far back had it diverged from the known species? Was it more closely related to the giant squid or to an octopus? She had so many questions, and so few data. She despaired of ever getting a sample of the tentacle thing without a suicide mission.

"Before we disperse," said Jules with a hand up. "Can we agree to change the name of the tentacle thing? No offense, Corrie, but it sounds like a name a toddler would come up with."

"What's your suggestion?" Corrie shot back, feeling both defensive and amused. Tentacle thing wasn't the greatest moniker, she had to admit—to herself, at least.

"Don't we have better things to do?" said Zeb. "Prepare for our rescue, for example?"

"Don't be so serious," said Jules. "This is important. Are we really going to let 'tentacle thing' be the name recorded in the history books? All in favor of 'Sucker' as a name, raise your hand."

"Sucker?" said Corrie. "What, because of the suction cups?"

Krista's hand rose to join Jules. To Corrie's surprise, so did Zeb's.

"Sorry, Corrie," Zeb said with a sheepish expression. "Jules won't let it go until we vote, so I thought I'd speed things up."

"And you're terrible at naming things," Krista added. "Spiky? Tentacle thing? Sucker's not much better, but it will do."

"Fine." Corrie threw her hands up in surrender. "Now, let's go make our slime grenades."

Corrie, Jules, and Krista traipsed through the cabin, leaving Zeb to drive the boat. Jules stopped in the galley to rummage through a cupboard. He emerged, triumphant, with a package of seaweed for wrapping sushi.

"How about this for a grenade wrapping?" he said. "We could mix the slime with sushi rice so it's not as wet. The nori will hold its shape until it hits the water, then it will fall apart and release the slime rice."

"Perfect," Corrie said. This was why she didn't like working alone in the lab. More brains meant more ideas. "My idea was to poke holes in a plastic bag when we were ready to throw it. We probably would all be writhing on the deck, hallucinating. Your idea is much better."

"Were you really planning on making sushi?" said Krista.

"As a final night treat," said Jules with a shrug. "We'll have to have something else, now."

"If we save the unicorn fish, I'll buy us all dinner," Corrie promised.

"Then our plans had better go swimmingly," Jules said with a grin. Corrie chuckled.

"You did not go there," said Krista, rolling her eyes. "Go on, cook up some rice. Corrie and I will collect slime."

Corrie took her cue and retreated to the lab. What would she need for collecting slime from the unicorn fish? She opened drawers, thinking. Her equipment was laid out neatly, strapped down in baggie envelopes she had made on the first day. An eyedropper caught her eye. She slid it out of its envelope and took a few long swabs and sample bags for good measure.

On the deck, she kneeled beside the tank and removed the shade cloth. Krista squatted beside her.

"You're not going to hurt it, are you?" Krista said with an attempt at indifference, but there was a thread of worry threaded between her words. Corrie shook her head.

"No, we won't need to. Spiky is safe from us." She lifted the lid and admired the fish's iridescent skin under its coating of glutinous slime. There was a thin layer of excretions at the bottom of the tank already, and Corrie pointed at it.

"Can you suck up the bottom slime with the eyedropper and put it in a bag?" Corrie said. "Don't forget your gloves."

"We don't have time for visions today," said Krista. She put on a pair of gloves with an efficient snap, then frowned at Corrie. "What are you going to do? Am I just your science lackey now?"

Krista's mouth held no hint of humor, but her eyes were lively. Corrie grinned, surprised and pleased at Krista's banter.

"I've always wanted one. But they're called assistants. Or work-study students." She put on her own pair of gloves then held up a swab. "I'm going to take a bit of fresh slime off Spiky, just in case freshness is important. We'll mix it all together so that every grenade has some fresh slime in it."

Krista eyed the swab with suspicion.

"Be gentle."

"Don't worry," Corrie said. "I'm not Matt."

It was late afternoon by the time the *Clicker* turned into the mouth of a narrow inlet. The sun was still high, but it couldn't peek over the steep cliffs of the fjord, and all but the

192

highest rockfaces were dim and cool. Corrie shivered and zipped up her jacket. Jules came out with a sandwich wrapped in a napkin and handed it to her.

"What's this?" Corrie said.

"It's almost dinner, and we don't have time for a proper meal. Sorry, it's just a sandwich."

Corrie laughed. He was sorry for only making a sandwich? She had completely forgotten about food.

"That was sweet of you, thanks. We could have eaten later."

"Miss dinnertime?" Jules said in mock-outrage. "How are we supposed to keep up our strength? Sacrilege. I'll pretend you didn't say that."

Corrie grinned and took a big bite of the bread. She chewed thoughtfully.

"Hey, look what I rigged up," Jules said. He bent down and picked up something from the deck. It was made of what looked like a small fishing net with the netting cut away. Instead, a bungee cord was tied to either side of the metal loop. In the middle of the bungee cord was an egg cup from the galley.

"A new way to cook eggs?" Corrie said with a raised eyebrow.

"No, it's a slingshot," Jules said with excitement. "I've been practicing. My job is to throw slime grenades into the water if we need to call Sucker, right? I have a crappy throwing arm—I was never much good at sports—but my aim with this thing is pretty good. It gets my shots way farther. Here, watch."

Jules took an egg from his pocket and fitted it into the egg cup. He pulled back, closed one eye and tightened his lips as he aimed, then he released the egg cup. The egg soared away in a long arc, until it finally plopped with a splash in the quiet waters of the inlet.

"Nicely done," Corrie said, impressed. "It reminds me of

193

something my dad would create. MacGyver was his hero. Your slingshot would definitely win points with him."

"Here's hoping I don't need to use it." Jules' usual grin faded. "How big was Sucker, again?"

"I hope you don't have to use it, too," Corrie said by way of an answer. Refreshing Jules' memory on Sucker's size wouldn't help anyone, herself included. "We'll sneak in, take the unicorn fish to the water, release them, and sneak out again. No one will see. It will all be fine."

Jules gave her a skeptical smile.

"Yeah. Just like that."

Krista came to the aft deck and stood beside them. She was dressed in tight-fitting exercise pants and a dark shirt with running shoes.

"Going for a jog?" Jules asked.

"No, doofus. What if we need to run or fight? I want to have full range of motion."

Corrie swallowed and looked at her own ensemble of jeans and T-shirt. Was she ready for anything? She was more worried about the readiness of her mental state than her clothing. By the look of her, Krista was prepared in both ways.

"We're almost there," Krista said. "We're going to anchor the *Clicker* around the next bend and take the dinghy from there. Get the winch ready."

"Get the winch ready yourself," said Jules, but he followed Krista to the winch, and they started to clear the dinghy's path. Corrie took a deep breath to steady herself. How could she prepare for the unknown? She walked into the lab. There must be something she could take to equip herself for whatever scenario they might come across.

A few minutes later, a clanking alerted Corrie to the anchor descending. She put a final piece of equipment in her pocket and walked out of the lab, feeling better about their upcoming mission.

"What the hell is all that?" Krista said when she spotted her. Corrie stuck out her chin in defiance.

"Equipment. You never know what we might need."

After Krista shrugged and turned away, Corrie looked down at her waist. From a makeshift belt, she had hung an assortment of useful items. Some were taped to the belt, like the sheath of her scalpel, while others were inside sample bags or plastic test tubes attached to the belt by twist ties. She was quite proud of her utility belt, but an objective side of her brain recognized how ridiculous she looked. She tossed her head. If she used even one item from the belt, it would be worth it.

Zeb gave her belt a double-take when he emerged from the wheelhouse, but he made no comment. Corrie, recovered from Krista's scorn, decided to show it off.

"What do you think?" she said, strutting down the deck. "It's the latest in lab fashion. All the Nobel prize winners are wearing one."

Zeb snorted, and Corrie felt a twinge of pride for breaking his usual calm expression.

"Come on," Krista called from the dinghy, now bobbing in the water beside the *Clicker*. "Let's get this show on the road."

"After you." Zeb gestured toward the ladder. "I don't want to risk lab equipment falling on my head."

"Oh, you have no idea," she said playfully. "I am a lethal weapon right now."

Instead of sitting next to the motor as Corrie had expected, Zeb sat in the middle and fitted oars into the oarlocks.

"Old school rowing?" she asked as she settled herself in the bow, the only place left in the tiny boat. Krista and Jules were already squished together in the stern and not looking particularly happy about it.

"It's quiet." Zeb started to pull the oars with long, confident strokes. "This is a covert operation, after all."

195

Corrie turned her body to watch where they were going. Jellyfish drifted by the boat under the surface, looking like little moons in a deep green sky. A waterfall cascaded down a sheer cliff in front of them and splashed into the calm water below.

Zeb kept to the side of the inlet, close enough to see emerald green moss clinging to the rockface. An arbutus tree grew horizontally out of the cliff far above them and Corrie wondered how it retrieved nutrients or water from the inhospitable rock. It seemed impossible to survive, and yet, the tree thrived.

Corrie scanned the inlet in front of them. When a dwelling met her eye, she hissed in shock.

"There's a house!" she called back. "Is that it?"

"Must be," Krista said. Her eyes narrowed when she spotted it. "It's the only habitation on this section of the inlet. Careful, Zeb."

"What do you want me to do?" Zeb said with an exasperated tone. "Row more quietly?"

"The *Defiance* is there, too," Jules said. His voice was subdued. Corrie glanced at his pale face in concern. "Matt must be at home."

Krista swore. Then she looked thoughtful.

"Maybe it's for the best," she said. "If we meet him, we can show that bastard what we really think of him."

"Or not," Corrie squeaked. She cleared her throat. "Let's keep trying the sneaky way, okay? Maybe he's sleeping. Or he went for a walk."

"On all those hiking trails?" Krista said with an eyebrow raised at Corrie's suggestion. Corrie looked again.

The cabin was a tiny affair, made of rough-hewn logs and a corrugated metal roof. It sat right on the edge of the water on a tiny peninsula of land. The cabin almost filled the entire shelf of exposed rock, which ended at the cliff face. Unless Matt liked to rock climb or swim, there was nowhere to go.

Corrie started to sweat.

"Row to the cave," Jules said to Zeb. "We can keep the dinghy out of sight there. Assuming he isn't watching us right now."

Zeb nodded and kept rowing. The muscles of his arms tightened his shirt sleeves with the motion. Slowly, so slowly, they floated toward the cave on the left side of the cabin. It was no more than a dark gash in the side of the cliff, but the *Defiance* was tied up to a small dock inside it.

Somehow, they glided into the cave with no movement from the cabin. Corrie let out a sigh of relief when the dinghy nudged against the dock.

"Do you have your grenades?" she whispered to Jules. He nodded tightly.

"Don't mess up, doofus," Krista said. "But we probably won't need you, anyway. You just relax here and let the adults do the dirty work."

Zeb shot Krista a look, then he turned to Jules.

"Remember, only use the grenades as a last resort. We don't know what Sucker will do when it's called. Only if you think we really need the distraction, okay? But we might need it if Matt is here, so keep a close eye."

Jules gave his friend a wan smile and waved them off.

"Go rescue your salty damsels in distress."

Zeb led the way up the rocky path. The cabin's few windows were grimy, and they could see no movement in them. Zeb held a finger to his lips and waved them forward. Krista huffed in annoyance and pushed past Zeb to walk toward the cabin. Corrie gulped then followed. There was a difference between brave and foolish, and Krista was veering toward the foolish side. Would it hurt her to be a little more

197

cautious?

Zeb clearly thought the same, for he exchanged a resigned look with Corrie as they followed his sister on silent footfalls. Krista flattened herself against the wall beside a window and peered inside. Corrie's fingernails bit into her palms, but she joined Krista at the window.

Nobody was inside. Corrie let out a breath she hadn't realized she was holding. Now that immediate danger was out of the way, she allowed herself to look around with astonishment. A large table dominated the middle of the room. It was covered in a haphazard array of equipment. Corrie recognized some bottles of chemicals, hydrochloric acid and ethanol among them. There was a fridge, a specialized container full of what Corrie knew to be liquid nitrogen, and a small oven. But what really drew Corrie's attention was the row of six large aquarium tanks lined up against the far wall. In four of them swam four unicorn fish of varying sizes. They moved in slow circles, and some showed clear signs of damage on their flanks.

"What is he doing to them?" Krista hissed. "Look at them. They're all mangled."

"He's collecting slime," Zeb said calmly from behind them. "It's probably freshest if he scrapes it off their bodies."

Corrie turned to look at Zeb in horror. Although his voice was calm, his eyes showed dangerous emotion below the surface. He met her gaze and nodded.

"Let's get them," he said. "It's time."

"All right," Krista said. "I'm first."

She marched around the corner. Corrie followed with her heart in her throat. Fear pounded in her chest like an animal clawing its way out, but indignation for what Matt was doing spurred her forward. Not only was he capturing never-before-studied animals for his own gain, he was abusing them. They had to stop it. She thought fleetingly of the police but couldn't even begin to imagine how that would work.

198

Besides, her secret of the unicorn fish would escape. Not that the fish weren't more important, of course they were, but if they could solve it on their own without alerting the authorities, then everyone would benefit. Except Matt, of course. That bastard could rot in hell, for all Corrie cared. She smiled to herself at channeling her inner Krista.

Krista eased the door open. It creaked loudly and they all froze. When nothing moved, Krista slipped inside the gap and Zeb and Corrie followed. Eight fish eyes gazed at them. A strange, chemical smell permeated the air, and aquarium pumps hummed and bubbled. They were in.

Corrie whipped out three pairs of gloves from one of her makeshift pouches and passed them around.

"Here. Put these on and grab yourself a fish."

"Just toss them outside into the water?" Zeb said.

"Unless you have a better idea," said Krista. She peered through the glass of the nearest tank and her expression softened. "Poor little guys. Let's get them out of here."

"You're not touching anything," said a voice behind them. Corrie's entire body stiffened, and her heart nearly stopped. Krista jumped and Zeb's eyes grew wide. They turned toward the voice.

Matt stood at a doorway that had been closed at the back of the cabin. His face was puffy and his hair tousled as if he had been sleeping, but his narrowed eyes were alert.

"Back away from the fish and get out of my cabin. I don't know how you found this place, and I don't care. Leave now before I make you."

Krista planted her feet apart and crossed her arms. The thin white gloves she wore should have been comical, but Corrie found nothing to laugh at.

"We're releasing the fish, and you're stopping this druggie shit. Right now."

"You have nothing on me," Matt sneered. "You think you can make me do anything?"

199

"Three of us and one of you," Zeb pointed out, in a tone he might use for announcing the weather forecast. Matt laughed loudly.

"Yeah, pretty terrifying."

"Does your girlfriend know?" Krista said with a tilt to her head. Corrie was amazed by her poise. Krista might be prickly, but she shone in confrontation. Jules had mentioned that she was a lawyer—Corrie hoped she never had to be on the opposite side of her in court. Matt grimaced, then his face purpled.

"You leave Bianca out of this," he growled.

"Oh, we will." Krista waved to Corrie to scoop out a fish. Corrie put her hand over the tank. "As soon as we release the fish."

"Like hell you will." Matt lunged toward them, and the room went mad.

Zeb leaped at him. Matt swung a punch at Zeb's face, which he dodged. Krista kicked Matt in the side of the knee, and he went down in a grunt of pain only to lumber back up toward Zeb.

"Krista!" Corrie screamed. "Get the fish, then we can get out of here!"

Krista plunged her hands into the tank nearest the door and gripped a fish between her hands. She stumbled toward the door. Corrie dodged the grappling men and headed for a tank of her own. There was a splash, and Krista stumbled back in. Her face was white.

"Corrie," she gasped. "Gloves aren't enough. My arms got wet, and I rubbed my face by accident—oh, no—get away!"

Krista sank to her knees and scrabbled away from something that only she could see. Corrie's heart sunk. Slime must have entered her mouth, and now she was having visions. Krista was out of the running, and only she and Zeb were left to defend the fish—and themselves.

Zeb was on the floor gasping, with Matt pinning him from

above. Corrie didn't think. Her hand fumbled in a tube on her belt and extracted five long pipettes, glass tubes for measuring solutions. She banged them against the table edge and the ends shattered, leaving five jagged tips. Before she could overthink her actions, she plunged them into Matt's back.

They didn't go in far, but it was enough. Matt arched backward in pain, and Zeb wriggled free. He and Corrie ran behind the table to regroup.

"Got to take him down before we do anything," Zeb gasped. Corrie nodded frantically.

"Okay, there's lots to work with here." She glanced at the table in front of her, but they didn't have any more time to consider their options. Matt came around the table with his hands outstretched. Corrie threw off the lid of the liquid nitrogen container, heaved the container in her arms, and sloshed it toward their attacker.

Clouds of nitrogen turned from liquid to gas and billowed to the floor. Matt shrieked in pain as the intensely cold liquid hit his skin and left red welts where his hands and neck were exposed. Quickly, before he could recover, Corrie tossed a handful of tiny glass beads onto the floor from a bag on her belt.

Matt took a step forward, directly onto the beads. With a swift, scrabbling motion, his foot slid out from under him and he landed on his bottom. Corrie took a length of tubing from her belt and handed it to Zeb, then grabbed a glass flask from the table and smashed it so that only the jagged neck was left.

"I always wanted to do that," she said to Zeb. He was about to answer, then his face dropped in horror.

"Shit. Jules summoned Sucker."

201

JULES

Jules had no desire to confront Matt. He was quite happy to guard the dinghy and throw slime grenades if need be, Krista's snide comments aside. He wasn't designed for rescue missions.

But when the other three disappeared into the cabin and there was a moment of complete silence, Jules' conviction wavered. What was worse, confronting Matt and the dangers he embodied, or enduring the silence of waiting and not knowing?

A moment later, Jules realized that there was something worse than both those options. Shouts and banging erupted from the cabin. Jules gripped his makeshift slingshot in terror and indecision. What was happening? Was someone hurt? Jules remembered Matt's muscled frame and pitiless face, and he shuddered. Maybe he should go and help.

But what could Jules really do, beside presenting himself as cannon fodder? He'd never fought anyone in his life, not even as a child. His easy words and placating manner always diffused situations. He had no real skills. He would probably just mess things up. It would be better for everyone if he stayed out of it.

There was a crash of glass and a scream. Krista flung open the door with a wriggling bundle in one arm. She rubbed her face with her free hand and ran two steps to the water's edge. She stumbled, and the fish under her arm slid out of her hands and into a tiny tidepool, unconnected to the waters of the inlet. The horn of the unicorn fish shone in the dim light as it poked out of the water.

Krista's body shook, and she stumbled back indoors as if blind. When another shriek echoed through the door, Jules stood. His hands trembled with fear, but he couldn't sit inactive in the dinghy any longer. He glanced at the bucket of slime grenades at his feet. The crash of broken glass sounded again. Surely now they needed a distraction. Jules couldn't do much, but he could do this.

Jules picked up a slime grenade with a gloved hand. The nori was delicate yet still dry, and he hoped it would stay intact during its flight. He fitted it into the egg cup and pulled the bungee cord of his slingshot taut. He aimed at the water in front of the cabin, let out a breath, and released.

ZEBALLOS

Corrie's face paled before she whipped around to look through the front door, but Zeb only had eyes for what was outside. A lawn chair flew past the doorway and hit the cabin with a loud bang, and the sea frothed and roiled. Three massive tentacles reached through the white foam, writhing in fury. They felt blindly toward the cabin. One found the open door and wrapped itself around it. The suction cups gripped tightly.

The door ripped off its hinges with a shriek of bending metal and splintering wood.

"What the fuck is that?" Matt shouted behind Zeb. Zeb didn't have any focus to spare for their opponent. He threw a panicked glance at Corrie.

"Now what?" he said as they backed away from the door.

"Is there another way out of here?" Corrie said. Her voice was high-pitched. "The front door appears to be out of commission."

Another tentacle snaked around the doorframe and patted the ground, coming further and further into the cabin. Zeb nearly tripped on a chair in his hurry to escape.

Bang!

Gunshot deafened Zeb for a moment. He crouched down in fear and whirled around to find the source. Matt stood in the doorway of the bedroom with a hunting rifle in his hands. He looked wide-eyed but satisfied.

The tentacle slithered and flailed. Blood seeped out of a small wound in its flank. The tentacle retreated, and there was a moment's peace.

"I don't know what the hell that was, but it's gone now," Matt said. "Now, about you three. Are you still interested in fighting this mismatched bout?"

A tremendous thud shook the walls of the cabin. Zeb

turned to the door. Five tentacles wrapped around the doorframe and pulled remorselessly at the wall. The cabin groaned with the strain. Logs splintered, ripped, and tore apart.

Corrie shrieked and ran toward Krista, who was huddled on the floor in the corner of the cabin. She dragged the muttering woman out of reach of the sagging roof. Gunfire sounded again.

Matt shot at the tentacles, but his aim was wild with his fear. One ricocheted off the wall and slammed into the nearest tank. The glass shattered and water poured out of the side. The unicorn fish flopped in panic.

"Stop, you idiot!" Zeb yelled. He turned and charged toward Matt. His only thought was to wrestle the gun out of Matt's unruly grip. No good would come out of a stray bullet in someone's leg.

He slammed into Matt's side. The gun went off again, at the ceiling this time. Matt fell to the floor with Zeb on top of him, but a swift elbow to the face sent Zeb sprawling. Zeb kicked toward Matt in a desperate attempt to make contact, and his foot sent the gun skittering across the floor.

A sudden whoosh drew both their eyes. Corrie held an empty bottle of ethanol in one hand and backed away from a line of fire that crawled across the floor and up the splintered wall like an orange stain. Tentacles writhed in pain from the flames.

Zeb heaved himself up and chased after the gun while Matt stared dumbfounded at Corrie's conflagration. When his fingers touched the cool metal, he hesitated. Should he try to threaten Matt with it? He remembered Krista's advice after she had come home from a self-defense lesson when they were teenagers. "Don't bother with a weapon if you're more inexperienced. Your attacker can get the weapon from you easily, and then you'll be facing a guy with a weapon instead of just a guy."

Zeb raced around the table before Matt could get to his feet and opened a grimy window. There was just enough room to toss the rifle out the opening. Behind him, Matt growled with rage.

"Back off," Corrie yelled. Zeb spun around. Corrie held out a bottle of something labeled hydrochloric acid. "Back off or I'll douse you. Trust me, it will hurt."

Krista stood beside Corrie now, her face pale but determined. The small amount of drug must have worn off quickly, although her eye still twitched involuntarily.

The tentacles had retreated in the face of the fire, but the flames were out now, the ethanol burned off. The brigar would be back. They couldn't keep fighting a battle on two fronts. Now that Krista was recovered, she and Corrie could take on Matt. Krista could handle herself, he knew, and Corrie was proving resourceful. Zeb was their best chance at diverting the brigar. But how? Zeb's eyes fell on the gasping unicorn fish in the broken tank.

"I'll distract Sucker," he shouted. "Keep Matt busy."

"Zeb," Krista yelled hoarsely. "Get back here!"

Zeb seized a plastic bag nearby, scooped the fish into it, and sprinted for the door.

The brigar was wounded, but not out of the fight. A piece of charred tentacle lay sizzling beside Zeb's feet. Three more tentacles waved from the ocean, gathering speed, preparing to attack again. The brigar was infuriated now, and hellbent on taking back the strolias.

Zeb kicked off his sandals and dived into the water. It was an awkward dive with his plastic-wrapped bundle, but it got him in the water, and that was the important thing. His clothes chafed and hampered the flow of water across his skin. They prevented him gaining a full picture of his surroundings, but he didn't have time nor hands to remove them.

The water of the inlet was clearer than he had expected—freshwater runoff must flow into the fjord—and the brigar was hard to miss. Zeb almost choked on seawater. The brigar was shaped like a bulbous, flaccid octopus, but monstrously huge. The body was twice the length of Zeb, and the tentacles reached through the water and far into the sky above. Its alien eye, bigger than Zeb's head, looked angry and wild. The brigar was focused on the fight above and had little attention to spare Zeb. He was enormously thankful for that and wondered if this was the most sensible plan he could have thought of.

Zeb swam away from the cabin. If nothing else, he could distract the brigar from Krista and Corrie. He wouldn't be able to live with himself if he didn't at least try to do that. He wanted to be far enough away to make a difference, though.

The skin on his bare hands sensed a change. Zeb looked back. The brigar had brought all its tentacles into the water and was looking in his direction. Zeb's eyes drifted to the bag he carried. A river of slime water flowed out of a hole in the bag. The brigar stiffened, all eight of its arms frozen. Then, it shot toward Zeb with its tentacles flowing behind it.

Zeb untwisted the plastic bag with frantic fingers. The unicorn fish, previously in shock from its rough treatment and the frantic jostling in the bag, saw light and bolted. It thrashed out of the bag, tearing it on its way out, and raced away. Zeb pointed his head to the depths and swam as fast as he could without his flippers.

The nearest arm of the brigar lashed out. With inhuman dexterity and unerring aim, the end of the tentacle wrapped gently around the fleeing strolia. As soon as the suckers clasped the strolia's scales, the fish fell limp. Was it rendered unconscious, or was it simply relieved? Gently, the giant octopus drew the strolia into its body. When it released its tentacle, the fish clung to the smooth skin of the brigar's body. For the first time, Zeb noticed other strolias attached, so that the brigar appeared to be covered in spines.

Its task done, the brigar turned back toward the cabin. Zeb panicked. He had distracted it for hardly any time at all. He made a low moaning noise followed by a series of clicks. An octopus near his house that he was friendly with often responded to the noises he could make, taught to him by his mother. Maybe he could distract the brigar in the same way.

The monstrous octopus paused briefly then continued toward the shore. Zeb kicked with all his might. He had to help Krista and Corrie. They were between an enraged drug producer and a murderous sea monster. Zeb couldn't do much to help, but he could be by their side.

CORRIE

Matt eyed the bottle of hydrochloric acid warily. Corrie brandished it at him.

"I don't want to hurt you," she said.

"Much," Krista added.

"Just back off and let us release the fish, okay?" said Corrie. Matt's sneering face didn't look like he was interested in surrendering, but she had to try. "Then we can deal with the monster outside and get away with our lives." Fear flashed through her, but for Zeb, not herself. How did he think he would distract Sucker?

"Not a chance," Matt snarled. "This is my big ticket. My chance to get the money I'll never make otherwise. Get away from them!" This last was directed at Krista, who had run to the tanks and was carefully scooping out a unicorn fish with a nearby net. Krista gave him the finger and ran to the door. Corrie waved the bottle at Matt again.

Matt grabbed a garbage bag from the table and held it up like a shield then edged toward the tanks. Corrie shouted in alarm and threw the acid at his legs. The liquid only reached his boots, where it slid off the heavy leather without damage to the material.

Corrie looked around frantically. What else could she use to keep the large man at bay? The light of a small oven winked on. She pulled on oven mitts from the overflowing table, flung the oven door open, and took out an oven rack. She ran toward Matt, who was almost at the tanks, and screamed in defiance. Matt, who was focused on the returning Krista, barely had a chance to put up an arm in defense before Corrie slammed the hot metal against his shoulder. It melted the plastic bag and seared through Matt's cotton shirt, and he roared in pain.

Krista scooped out another unicorn fish and ran to the

door. Before she could go through, five giant tentacles reared up from the water. Krista screamed and backed away.

"Throw the fish in!" Corrie yelled. "That's what Sucker wants!"

Krista wound the net up and flung the contents toward Sucker. The unicorn fish went flying, but it didn't hit the water. One of Sucker's arms deftly caught the squirming fish and tucked it into the sea with hardly a splash.

Krista sprinted back, but she was on the wrong side of the room. Matt was at the last tank, one frantic-looking fish inside, with Corrie and her oven rack in front of him. How would they get the last fish?

Krista picked up a laboratory-grade water bath and threw it to the floor. It smashed into three pieces with a resounding crack. Matt winced. Then, his face purpled with rage.

"That was a thousand dollars!" he shouted. Krista shrugged.

"Whoops." She picked up a tray of flasks and deliberately dropped the whole thing. The shattering sprayed glass all over the floor.

"Give it up," Corrie said. She tossed her now-cool oven rack aside. It bounced off the floor with a dull clang and came to rest beside the broken tank. She withdrew her scalpel with one hand. The other hand picked up a glass flask and broke the bottom off. It was a terrible waste of lab equipment, of course, but damn if it didn't feel good to be a little destructive after so many months of utmost care in her university lab.

"Never," Matt said, but that was his final word. Quicker than a shark, a massive tentacle swatted Matt to the ground like Corrie might a pesky wasp. It gently curled around the final unicorn fish in its tank and hauled it out of the ruined cabin. Corrie's gaze followed the tentacle as it slid back into the water. It left only ripples in its wake.

Corrie looked with wide eyes at Krista, whose tanned face was pale with shock.

"Do you think Sucker knows it has them all?" Corrie said. Krista shrugged, her eyes scanning the jagged opening where the door used to be.

"Time will tell," Krista said. She walked over to Matt, who was groaning on the floor amid shards of glass and broken equipment. His clothes were ripped, burned, and eaten away, and he was bleeding in a few places. Corrie couldn't find it in herself to muster up much sympathy. Krista kicked him over. Matt moaned when glass pressed into his back, and he struggled to sit up.

A commotion at the entrance made Corrie's heart leap in her chest—surely Sucker wasn't back for more—but it was only Zeb outlined against the orange light of the unseen sunset. He was soaking, and his shirt clung to his chest and dripped onto the floor.

"Why are you wet?" Corrie said in bewilderment. "And where are your shoes? Did Sucker pull you in? How did you escape? Watch out for the glass, it's everywhere. And—"

"Everything's fine," Zeb said over her words. She clamped her mouth shut. It was such a relief to have Sucker gone, the unicorn fish out, Matt on the floor, and now Zeb in one piece, that she was having trouble containing herself. Zeb gave her a half-smile, which Corrie figured translated to a broad grin in anyone else. "Sucker swam away. It's done."

Corrie let out her breath in a long, slow sigh. Her knees trembled. Now that the fight was over, adrenaline wasn't supporting her. She gritted her teeth and promised herself she wouldn't fall over.

"Are you okay?" Zeb said with concern in his voice. Corrie waved him off.

211

"Fine, fine. A couple of cuts, mainly self-inflicted. You should see the other guy." She grinned. "Matt got it worse."

Zeb's eyes flickered to Matt, now propped on his feet against the wall nearest the opening with an irate Krista close by, holding a broken flask in front of her.

"You know this was a stupid idea, right, Matt?" Krista said with disdain. "Drugs, really? And from something you have no idea about?"

"It was fine until you people showed up," he muttered. He glared up at Krista. She glared back, undeterred.

"Bet you didn't expect Sucker to come around, did you? That's what you get for meddling in crap you know nothing about."

"Oh, and you do?" he shot back.

"I know enough to tread carefully, yes. I pride myself on not being an idiot."

"Why did you do it?" Corrie asked. "This is a big setup for one guy, and lots of risk. What did you need the money for so badly?"

Matt shrugged then winced from the motion.

"My girlfriend, Bianca, she deserves more than what I've got. I'm saving up for a ring, you know? And why can't we go to Vegas like Stacy?" He stared into the distance through the ruined wall of the cabin. Corrie frowned.

"Would she really want you to make money like this, though? Drugs, exploitation of dangerous animals, all this? Surely, she would rather have a happy boyfriend with a respectable job, instead of all this." Corrie waved around the cabin. Matt laughed. There wasn't much mirth in the sound.

"She's not that kind of woman."

Corrie crossed her arms.

"Then maybe she's not worth it," she said. "Not everyone is." She should know. Her ex Dylan wasn't, that's for sure. When she had finally left him, and gotten through her meltdown after, she'd never looked back. It was painful to

212

see someone make similar mistakes.

Matt stared at her for a moment. What was he thinking? She hoped he was reevaluating his priorities. She really didn't want to have a repeat of this showdown in his new drug lab somewhere.

Matt's eyes narrowed for a spilt second, and that was Corrie's only warning. He kicked an empty bottle at Krista, who swore and grabbed her bruised shin. Zeb shouted, but Matt threw a splintered board from the doorframe at him, and Zeb had to duck to avoid it. Corrie started forward without a clear plan, but Matt took off with a limping run toward the dock.

"Jules is down there," Zeb said, and he raced after Matt.

Corrie ran after him. Running was too generous a word— it was more of a hobble. She thought they were done with fighting. Her body had already packed in for the day and was ready to collapse with a stiff drink in hand.

It was only a few dozen paces to the dock. Zeb stopped at the edge. Jules was in the dinghy staring at Matt, who started the engine of the *Defiance* with a frenzied expression. The engine turned over a few times until it finally caught with a grumble. Krista pelted up beside Corrie as the *Defiance* backed away from the dock.

"Don't you ever try that shit again!" Krista yelled after Matt. "We'll be watching!"

Matt ignored her and turned the nose to the mouth of the inlet. He roared away without a backward glance.

Jules whistled.

"Is that it? Did you do it?" he asked.

"Yeah." Zeb had a genuine smile on his face this time. "We all did. Unicorn fish are back in the water."

"Lab destroyed and messaged to Matt delivered," Krista said with a smug nod.

"And Sucker's gone," Corrie added. "Nicely done summoning it, by the way, Jules. The slime grenades

213

worked."

"Like a charm." Jules brandished his makeshift slingshot then held up the bag of slime-rice balls covered with nori. "Snack, anyone?"

"We are not repeating your freak-out from the other day, dimwit," Krista told him. "Once was enough."

"We did it," Corrie said. She shook her head, marveling. Now that the danger was over, she could revel in their accomplishment. If this was scientific fieldwork, she was on board. "We saved the unicorn fish from exploitation. We stopped a fledgling drug trade. We discovered two new species, one of which is fricking ginormous. We totally rock, you guys."

Even Krista cracked a smile at Corrie's enthusiasm. The other two laughed aloud.

"Hop in, everyone," Jules said. "Back to the boat. It's time to celebrate."

"But no sushi," Corrie said with a glance at the slime grenade bag. Jules winked at her.

"No sushi. Scouts' honor."

Half of the sky glowed with a brilliant orange sunset covered by streaky pink clouds. The other half glittered with the emergence of the night's first stars. Corrie took a deep breath of cool, salty air that rushed past her. Jules drove the dinghy at top speed, occasionally twisting in snake-like curves for fun. Krista didn't even reprimand him, and Zeb gave him a fist-bump when Krista wasn't looking. Corrie giggled to herself and let her hair out of its braid. If there was ever a time to let her hair down, it was after a pitched battle with a sea monster. She felt herself on the edge of laughing hysterically and took another deep breath to calm herself. She turned to Jules.

"What sort of alcohol do you have on board?" she asked him. "I think we need to celebrate in a big way."

Jules flashed her a wicked grin.

"Don't worry, we're well stocked. Let it never be said that the Artinos kept a dry boat."

Zeb's mouth twitched, and Krista rolled her eyes.

"True enough. Dad would roll over in his grave if he thought we were teetotalers."

"Difficult to do when you're cremated," Zeb said. Corrie choked on her laugh in case he took offense. Was that a joke? Or was it too soon for Zeb? His crinkled eyes at her reaction relieved her.

"I'll make dinner," Jules announced once they were back at the *Clicker*. He looked them over with mock-derision. "You'd better all clean yourselves up, filthy laborers. Have you never heard of dressing for dinner?"

"Zeb," Corrie said in shock. "You're dripping, I forgot. Aren't you freezing? We could have found a blanket or something at the cabin. Why didn't you say?"

"I'm fine," he said quickly. "Look, I'll go change now. No worries."

He turned to disappear into the cabin. Corrie frowned after him, but she didn't miss the look that Krista and Jules exchanged before Krista went to the aft deck and Jules retreated to the galley. And, now that she thought about it, Zeb hadn't looked cold at all. No blue lips, no shivering, no goosebumps. He seemed comfortable, if anything. Maybe he was part beluga whale. She stifled a giggle. He didn't have enough body fat for that, that was sure. His clinging shirt told that story, even if she hadn't seen him in his bathing suit every day for the past week.

Corrie shook her head and walked into the lab. Her brain was jumping all over the place, not settling on anything, not even making much sense. She needed to clean up, eat, and relax with her boat mates. That would cure everything.

Krista's voice murmured from the aft deck. Corrie moved to the back door to investigate. Krista kneeled beside Spiky's tank with the shade cloth off and spoke in a low voice to the fish. Corrie tried to back away quietly—it was clear Krista was having a nice moment with the creature, which she had taken such a liking to—but Krista jerked her head to look at Corrie in surprise. Her face grew stony with embarrassment. Corrie put up her hands.

"Sorry for interrupting," Corrie said.

"There was nothing to interrupt," Krista said.

"It's not a big deal. I have a fish tank at home, you know. I talk to them all the time. My favorite is my pleco, Hot Lips. I swear he knows me and listens. I'm sure I'm making it up, but it's nice all the same."

Krista looked at Spiky with a softened expression.

"She does seem to listen."

"She?"

"It seemed nicer than calling Spiky an 'it.'"

"Oh, darn," said Corrie. "I thought maybe you'd found out the sex somehow. I was going to write down the info." Corrie paused, not wanting to break the news but knowing she had to. "Krista, we need to put Spiky back. Clearly, Sucker is looking for unicorn fish, and it's not right to keep her in a tank. I have plenty of data to analyze, and we can always put down the jellyfish bait if we need more specimens. I even have samples of slime in the freezer in case we ever want to summon Sucker. We should let Spiky go."

"I know." Krista sighed. "That's why I was saying goodbye." She coughed, as if realizing what she had just said, then she glared up at Corrie. "Don't you dare tell the boys that."

Corrie smiled.

"Mum's the word. Don't worry, I get it."

Corrie picked up a bucket and carefully scooped Spiky

216

into it. The fish glided calmly into the bucket, as if she knew what they were doing. Corrie hauled the bucket to the stern with Krista following.

"Ready?" Corrie asked her. Krista nodded.

"Do it."

Corrie dumped the contents of the bucket out. Water poured in a graceful arc from the bucket into the water. The unicorn fish dropped, sinuously twisting her body as she fell, the horn glinting in the last of the sky's orange glow. Then she splashed into the water, lost to sight. Krista sighed again.

"Can I ask you a question?" Corrie said.

"Sure."

"Why were you so hostile to me at the beginning? It was weird. Did I do something? You seem okay now."

Krista twisted her mouth as if she had swallowed something sour.

"It wasn't you, not really. It was what you represented. I didn't want Zeb chasing his dreams." A breath of air escaped Krista, and Corrie realized it was a rare laugh. "That didn't sound right. If he had ambitions, career dreams, I would never stand in his way. I respect that. But he's obsessed with storybook creatures, and I didn't want him wasting his life chasing those kind of dreams. Then you turned up and enabled his obsession. It was hard not to resent you."

Corrie nodded, but inside she wondered about Krista's statement. Why was Zeb obsessed with mythical creatures?

"I get it. There's a reason I'm anonymous online, with my blog. It's not something anyone normal should devote their lives to, right?"

"Yeah. He's my little brother, you know? But it's hard to look out for the idiot when he pulls stunts like this. But you know what? Sometimes dreams come true." Krista snorted at the cliché. "What do you know. Now he'll never let it go, but I can't blame you for that anymore, not when I've seen what I've seen. I guess we're all in it, now."

217

"Once you see it, you can't unsee it," Corrie said. "Hey, look."

Far in the distance, where the wake of their boat disappeared into the waves, a long tentacle emerged from the dark water. It was wreathed in the reflection of stars, and it twisted before sliding back into the darkness once more.

"Did it just wave at us?" Corrie said. It sounded silly out loud, but she had to say it.

"Don't be ridiculous." Krista softened the words with a smile. "Come on, let's see what Jules whipped up for a celebratory dinner."

ZEBALLOS

Zeb pulled the boat into a tiny bay that was tucked away on a small island. Not many boaters used it, and today was no exception. They were the sole inhabitants on the water, and the few cabins that ringed the shoreline were dark in the starlight. He dropped anchor in the middle of the bay.

Zeb was clean and dry now, after a toweling and a change of clothes before they left. Not that he minded being wet, but it had led to awkward questions from Corrie. Krista usually got after him for dripping on seats, so cleaning up was better all around. He hadn't felt the same desire to jump in the water again, despite being fully clothed during his dip with Sucker. Clothes were less constrictive than a wetsuit, certainly, and they must have allowed enough water movement over his skin to satisfy his body. Zeb still didn't understand it fully, but he appreciated not needing to pander to his body's unusual whims for once.

Once the boat was anchored, he found the others on the aft deck with beers in hand.

"Where's mine?" he said in greeting. Jules tossed him a can.

"Bottoms up. We're celebrating." Jules took a generous gulp of his own beer.

"What's for dinner tonight?" asked Corrie.

"Homemade lasagna," Jules said with a proud smile. "Only the best for my team of sea monster wranglers."

"I hope it's ready soon," said Krista. "I'm starving."

"Never satisfied, my malcontented crew member," Jules said.

"That's a big word for you. Sure you know how to spell it?"

"Why would I need to spell it, when I have a perfectly functioning mouth?" Jules retorted. He flapped his tongue at

Krista and Corrie burst into laughter. She looked good with a smile. The last couple of days had been so tumultuous and full of danger and work that Zeb hadn't seen Corrie lighthearted much, although he guessed that was her default mode. It suited her.

"I think we've earned lasagna," Zeb said to distract his sister and friend from harping on each other, even if it were mostly good-natured. "We've accomplished a lot this week. I propose a toast." He held up his can and the others mimicked him. "To new discoveries."

"To new discoveries," Jules and Corrie echoed. Krista was silent, but she drank along with the rest.

"We've found two new species," Zeb said. He was nervous about what he wanted to say, but it had to be said. Right here, right now, was an opportunity that he would never get again. He hoped the others felt the same way. "What else might be out there? The ocean is a deep and mysterious place."

"We know more about the moon than we do the ocean," Corrie said. Zeb nodded at her.

"Exactly. We found two new species in a week. Who knows what we could find if we kept searching? Corrie, I would like to offer an extension of another week to your award. For your science work as well as creature hunting. It doesn't have to be next week, but sometime soon. They're waiting for us."

Krista stared at him with hard eyes that didn't mask her concern, but Corrie's face lit up.

"Seriously?" She jiggled on the spot, seemingly unable to contain herself. "That's incredible. Another whole week. I'm seriously the luckiest student in the world. I'll need a couple of weeks—do some lab work, analyze what I have before we go out again—but oh, yes! I accept. A hundred times over." She grinned with unrestrained glee.

"What do you think, Jules?" Zeb asked his best friend,

who looked amused by Corrie's enthusiasm. "Are you up for another trip in a couple of weeks?"

"As long as you pay me," Jules said with an easy grin. "I'm game. We might talk about danger pay, though."

Zeb grinned back.

"We can talk about that."

"Really?" Krista said to him with a grimace. "You're going to keep doing this, aren't you?"

"Yep," said Zeb with finality.

"And nothing I say will dissuade you?"

"Nope."

Krista stared at him for a moment, then she released a long-suffering sigh.

"You're eating into my vacation time, boy. I only get so much as a junior attorney. You'd better visit me at Christmas this year. I'll be working Christmas Eve for sure."

"I will cook you turkey dinner," Zeb promised. "Or bring along a dinner that Jules cooked."

"Probably safer that way," Krista said. "I'm only agreeing because someone needs to keep you two weirdos in line, and although Corrie has proven her abilities in that regard, I don't want her to shoulder the burden alone."

Zeb was relieved, more than he could express, so he simply looked at his sister with grateful eyes. She rolled her own.

"Come on, Jules," she said. "Let's check your dinner. I can't wait any longer."

"Leave out some blue curacao and vodka," Corrie called after them. "I'll make my new specialty, the flaming narwhal."

Jules waved to indicate that he had heard, and they disappeared into the cabin. Corrie turned to lean against the railing. Zeb joined her, and they gazed out at the dark sea and diamond-studded sky.

"Flaming narwhal?" Zeb asked. Corrie giggled.

"I make crazy drinks for parties. Different colors, densities, sometimes fire—my dad taught me a lot of chemistry, and I like to make my skills transferable."

"I look forward to it."

"I could improve the flavor, honestly, but it looks amazing." Corrie looked up at the night sky. All traces of sunset had vanished long ago, and the moonless night was dark and cool. Zeb was mesmerized by the reflection of stars glimmering in Corrie's eyes. Water lapped quietly on the hull below them. Otherwise, they were immersed in peaceful silence.

"I don't know what to do about these creatures," Corrie said after a moment's pause. Zeb smiled to himself. He should have guessed that she wouldn't let silence reign for long. "I can't really tell my supervisor about them. We discovered two new species, but I don't have enough proof to show anyone yet."

"What about your data and samples? And don't forget the pictures."

Corrie looked undecided.

"It's a start, a necessary start, but a new species is big. Just because I have pictures and some DNA doesn't mean anything, really. Pictures can be doctored so easily. I really should have kept Spiky if I wanted to go there, but I don't, not yet. I don't know, Zeb. This is such a weird position to be in. My whole life, I've kept my fascination with legendary sea creatures a secret, separate from everything else, everyone else. Certainly, my science career and my creature blog only overlapped in that I used my scientific analysis skills to look at blog data. Otherwise, totally separate. Do I say anything to my supervisor? When do I say something?"

"Do you have enough data from your anemone project?" Zeb asked. He didn't like Corrie's uncertainty at telling her professor. If he had his way, only the four of them would ever know anything about strolias and brigars. They were from his mother's world of stories. He didn't want anyone else hunting and dissecting the creatures his mother had woven into her tales, not until he knew what he needed to know. He had thought that finding a strolia would tell him something, but it only brought up more questions than answers. He wanted—needed—to know more. Having teams of scientists combing the waters for his secrets would only make life more difficult.

"Oh, yes," said Corrie. "That's not a worry. It was a successful trip, even discounting our bonus finds. I don't have to make excuses."

"Then, keep it quiet for now," Zeb said, trying to sound disinterested. Corrie glanced at him, and he wondered how successful he had been at keeping the emotion out of his voice. "No harm. We can find out more before you take anything—" He swallowed. "Public."

"What's your stake in this?" Corrie asked. Zeb blinked. Corrie didn't dance around. What should he tell her? For one wild minute, he considered laying all his secrets bare. Common sense prevailed. Despite their intense time together, he had known Corrie for less than a week.

"My mother told me tales of the sea as a kid, and they've always fascinated me. And the ocean is such a vast place." He spread his arm out to showcase the waters surrounding them. "Who knows what's out there?"

None of that was a lie, but would it be convincing enough to satisfy Corrie? She smiled.

"We're starting to know, aren't we?" she said, and Zeb breathed a sigh of relief. "Although I don't know how we are finding these creatures so easily and yet they haven't been documented before. What are they doing, following us around? Are you the pied piper of fish?"

"I was wondering the same of you," Zeb said. "I've been on the water all my life, and I've never seen either creature. It's bizarre." Zeb frowned. Corrie was right. Why were the strolias so easy to find? They were rare enough that Larry and Matt could only catch them off the tip of Harwood Island, but Jules simply had to toss in a jellyfish-baited line anywhere and they caught one. And why was the brigar close enough to their boat to sense the strolia slime? Corrie interrupted his musings.

"You're probably right about not going public yet. Jonathan would run with it and leave me out of the loop, anyway." Corrie brooded for a moment. "Finding a new creature was my dream and my ticket to bigger things, if I'm being honest with myself. But now I can't use that information until we know more. Or maybe never, depending on what we find. Already, someone tried to exploit the unicorn fish. Maybe it's better that nobody knows. Except, if they were known, fisheries could be regulated and managed." She sighed. "It's a conundrum."

They stared at the water for several long beats. Corrie lapsed into an unusual silence. Zeb finally broke it.

"Did you ever think this would happen?" He meant finding strolias, a brigar, the whole mad thing. Corrie obviously knew what he meant.

"I hoped."

CORRIE

Zeb excused himself to help with dinner. Corrie watched the waves for a minute longer, mulling over decisions and species, but she wasn't a dweller by nature. She heaved herself off the railing, her entire body aching from the aftermath of their battle, and walked into the lab.

Her computer caught her eye, and she opened it to check her email. She hadn't sent her daily update to Jonathan yet. Jules would call her when dinner was ready, she was sure. She had time to dash off a quick message and attach her latest bit of data. She opened her mail.

A message waited from Robert, her friend in the sequencing lab. She held her breath and opened it.

Hi Corrie, I finally found primers that worked and got your samples sequenced. Hope you have a big wine budget for my speedy work. The results are weird, though. I ran one through the databases just for curiosity, and the matches it came up with were bizarre. Check it out.

There was an attached file. Corrie opened it and scanned the results with a frown. Robert was right. The unicorn fish wasn't coming up as any known species of salmon, although it was clearly related.

What was the unicorn fish? She knew it was different, but how? This was evidence, though, clear evidence that she had a new species. Corrie smiled and saved the file. She would do more work in the lab, gather more data, before she was ready to reveal her big find. If she did.

She shook her head to rid it her confusion and indecision and started an email for Jonathan. She dashed off a few inane remarks about the weather and sampling, then attached a couple of files that would show him her data. The data weren't pretty, but they would do for now. She'd be home in two days, and then the real work would start.

Jules' laughter filtered through the hallway. Corrie closed her laptop. That was enough about data and supervisors. It was time to celebrate. Those flaming narwhals wouldn't mix themselves.

ZEBALLOS

Zeb sat at the table feeling pleasantly buzzed. Jules had just stumbled off to his berth. Zeb wondered idly if he had made it into his bunk or was passed out on the floor. It wouldn't be the first time Zeb had heaved him into bed. Corrie and Krista had left a half-hour before. They were surprisingly chummy now, in that way women got sometimes, like they had been whispering secrets to each other and had inside jokes. Considering Krista's previous animosity, Zeb was surprised, or would have been if surprise could pass through his current cloud of alcohol-induced contentment.

It had been a good evening. Jules' lasagna was superb, of course, and Corrie's ridiculous flaming drinks were a hit. The flavor was disgusting, but Zeb drank it down in support. He wished he hadn't when Corrie only sipped at hers. She hardly drank anything, strangely, even though she was the life of the party. Jules drank like a fish, as usual, and Krista even lightened up to teach them a card game that was easy enough for Jules to learn in his state, and fast enough that they always beat him.

He should really go to bed—the sun would rise in a few hours at this time of the year—but he was enjoying his contentment so much that it was hard to force himself into the oblivion of sleep. He roused himself and wandered to the galley. A snack would be perfect right now. He had a craving for jellyfish, actually. Was there any left from making strolia bait? His craving grew stronger and he rummaged in the cupboards. There had better be some left. He was sure he had kept some for himself.

Ah ha, there it was. Zeb stuffed a piece in his mouth and chewed greedily. The jellyfish rolled over his tongue, the flavor salty and mild. He couldn't understand why the others turned their noses up at it. When he had a craving for it, nothing else would suffice.

His eye fell upon a stainless-steel bowl in the sink. Inside slouched the bag of slime grenades. Zeb slowed his chewing. They were the last remaining visible evidence of the strolias' existence on board. Zeb swallowed. What were the visions like? Despite having Jules for a friend, Zeb had tried very few illegal substances. Someone had to be responsible for Jules. The psychotropic substance from the strolias was from the world of his mother's stories. It was another clue, another piece of information about that world. How could he pass up a chance to learn more? Maybe the visions would tell him something important. How could he refuse?

He threw the jellyfish back in the cupboard and reached for the bowl. The nori was soft and soggy at this point, but Zeb forced himself to chew and swallow a whole ball. He washed his hands and sat down on the galley floor, wanting to be prepared for anything. Would the visions incapacitate him like they had Jules and Krista? He would try to be quiet, to not disturb the others. He didn't want them to know he was trying the slime.

Zeb waited for a vision. His heart pounded, but he didn't know if it was from the drug or his anticipation. A minute passed, then two. Five minutes later, Zeb leaped up and took another two grenades out of the bowl. He swallowed them as quickly as he could then sat back down.

Ten minutes later, he conceded defeat. The substance in the slime, the drug that had affected Jules and Krista so quickly and so violently, had absolutely no effect on him.

Why?

MATHIAS

Matt threw an empty beer bottle into the sea in a fit of rage. The *Defiance* bobbed gently in a calm bay that did not reflect Matt's mood at all. He couldn't go home tonight to see Bianca and be reminded of his failure, of all the things he could have given her and now were far out of reach. She would talk about Stacy and Las Vegas, no doubt, and the pictures of those damn rings would be tucked around the house everywhere. He couldn't face that yet.

It was over, though. What little money he'd managed to save up from his odd deckhand jobs had been spent on equipment for his lab, and thanks to that meddlesome bitch Krista and her merry band of do-gooders, it was all destroyed. Matt stormed into the galley and rummaged in the fridge for another beer. His hand clutched empty air. Even his beer was gone? He kicked the fridge in disgust, and his sore toes only worsened his mood.

Matt's eyes glanced at a box of baggies on the galley counter. They held three doses of Sea Salt, the last of his stores.

He hesitated for a moment then grabbed a baggie and opened it with shaking fingers. He might as well take it, for shits and giggles. The money from selling it would be a pittance, and Kiefer would be done with him if he couldn't provide a steady supply. Matt tipped the baggie into his mouth.

He nearly gagged from the taste, but he forced himself to swallow it. He could use an escape to make him forget about the whole mess. Maybe he would get a divine message to tell him how to turn his life around. He chuckled at the thought then stumbled outside.

The visions hit him like a wall of water. Tentacles rose from the depths, eerily like the ones that had attacked the

229

cabin earlier. Matt shrank against the cabin wall. The tentacles reached toward him, and one snaked around his torso before he could move. It dragged him remorselessly to the edge and over the railing. Matt screamed, but there was no one to hear his cries. With a sickening tilt, the ocean rose to meet his falling body.

Cold water surrounded him tightly like a vacuum-packed filet. Matt gurgled and tried to figure out which way was up. The tentacles were gone, and his head felt clear despite his panic. He kicked in a desperate attempt to reach the surface.

The muscles in his legs were hot. He shot forward through the water with speed disproportionate to his effort. Matt's eyes widened, and he almost forgot that he needed air. How had his legs grown so strong?

His lungs burned in reminder, and he kicked upward. He broke the surface with a tremendous leap to the sky. He gasped the clear night air in relief.

When he had caught his breath, he treaded water and thought. What had happened? Treading water had never been easier, and his speed in the water was insane. He'd been working out lately, but this was ridiculous.

The only thing different was his ingestion of Sea Salt. Had it caused the increased power in his muscles? He swam around to the engine and hauled himself on board. Immediately, his muscles weakened to normal strength.

Matt frowned and dipped a leg back in the ocean. When he kicked, his leg sliced through the water with ease.

Matt's mind sobered and churned with possibilities. Sea Salt caused hallucinations above water and increased strength below.

What would people pay for that?

JONATHAN

Jonathan Chang's phone beeped with a notification. He leaned over the side table to put on his reading glasses. His wife nudged him with her foot from her position on the couch.

"Are you watching our show or working?"

"I'll only be a minute," he said absently with his cell phone in hand. His wife shook her head and turned to the television. Jonathan opened his mail app and saw the offending email. Ah, from his student Corrie on the ship. It was about time. She was a terrible correspondent out there. Ships were always busy, he knew, but she could carve out time for important things like keeping her supervisor updated, surely.

He glanced over her message, which contained nothing of substance, then looked at the first file. It was a bar chart of salinities and temperatures from all of Corrie's stations. Jonathan sighed. There was nothing of interest here—it was simply supporting numbers for her relevant data, whenever she analyzed it. Typical students. They needed so much hand-holding. He was certain he had been far more driven and had showed more initiative during his graduate days.

There was one other file. Jonathan opened it, expecting another scintillating figure showcasing temperatures. Instead, it was a readout from sequencing analysis. Had Corrie sequenced some of her bacteria, sent her samples back to the university already? Jonathan felt an unexpected wave of admiration for his newest student, and his regard for her increased considerably. That was initiative.

But what was he looking at? These scientific names were not of bacteria. That was the family Salmonidae, containing Pacific salmon and trout. Why was Corrie analyzing fish genomes? Jonathan looked closer at the sample. It fit cleanly in the tree, nestled in the *Salmo* genus, but was different enough from the other species to warrant its own branch.

What had she found? An inkling of the importance of this figure dawned in Jonathan's mind. He thought for a moment.

"Are you done?" his wife said.

"Almost," he replied. He started a new email to a colleague.

What's the protocol for identifying a new species? What evidence is needed? Hypothetically speaking, of course.

Want to know more about the world of Clicker's stories?

I wrote a novelette called *Adrift* about an immortal magician living in the late nineteen-forties in Costa Rica who encounters sea creatures unlike any other. *Adrift* is free to subscribers of my newsletter.

As a subscriber, you'll also receive news about new releases, cover reveals, and giveaways exclusive to the newsletter. Be the first to know!

Visit **emmashelford.com** for your free book today.

ALSO BY EMMA SHELFORD

Nautilus Legends
Free Dive
More to come

Musings of Merlin Series
Ignition
Winded
Floodgates
Buried
More to come

Breenan Series
Mark of the Breenan
Garden of Last Hope
Realm of the Forgotten

ACKNOWLEDGEMENTS

Much thanks, as always, to Gillian Brownlee and Wendy Callendar for improving my books through their editing. Christien Gilston pulled off another fabulous cover. Thanks to Amanda Wells, Craig Richcreek, and Brandon Devnich for help with names. Captain Tim Bowles kindly contributed with nautical knowledge. Dr. Danielle Winget helpfully checked over the science for accuracy.

ABOUT THE AUTHOR

Emma Shelford is an author with an oceanography doctorate and the sea in her blood, which made writing the Nautilus legends such a delight. She is also the author of the Musings of Merlin series and the Breenan series.

Made in the USA
Columbia, SC
17 September 2019